To my dear wife, who is a true lady in every sense of the word.

Chapter One:
Alone

How long had it been raining? It seemed like weeks, but it had been only one day. Dark clouds boiled, and the rumble of thunder shook the house. The sound of heavy rain was followed by the drumbeat sound of hail hitting the roof. The wind began howling. It sounded like a freight train was about to run over the house. The storm had let up some, but it was still bad outside. It was only five in the evening, but the dark sky and cold wind made it feel much later.

She shivered under the blanket. The warmth of the empty house had quickly seeped out into the weather. There was no electricity, no natural gas, no kerosene for the lamps, and no candles. Fortunately, there was plenty of firewood. The coming night would not be cold enough to freeze but cold enough to make life miserable any distance from the fireplace. The new phone sat on a table in the front hall. It was completely dead. She was stuck in the middle of nowhere and had no idea what was actually going on or any way to reach out for help. She would have to figure out how to survive on her own.

Henrietta peeked out the window. The road was empty. No other houses were visible. The only food she had was the hard candy in her purse. She'd eaten all of it. Now she found herself sitting on a chair she'd pulled close to the fireplace. She stared into the flames of the slowly dying fire. The trip all the way from Britain had taken what seemed forever—days on a slow freighter, then more days on an uncomfortable train. Throughout the trip, she'd complained it would have been so much more fun if they had arrived by one of Baron Zeppelin's airships. Her cousin James considered that attitude ridiculous. Sure, there were a few airships in Europe that carried passengers, but they were small, fragile, and tended to catch fire. There was nothing like what Henrietta had imagined from reading fanciful accounts in the dime novels.

Henrietta was relieved when, finally, they had arrived. The sky was a terrific bright blue, having been scrubbed by the previous day's storms. There had been a two-seat steam runabout automobile waiting for them. Her uncle had arranged for the automobile to be left beside the station together with a note and a map. It warned that if bad weather required it, he and his house staff would go to a place he referred to only as "the Project." He instructed that if the house was empty, they should make themselves at home and await his return. He promised someone would check the house that evening. On finding the runabout, her cousin James insisted they drive out to the house. Ostensibly it was to "make sure it was still standing." In reality, he couldn't wait to drive the machine as fast as he could on the open, flat road. It was a pretty day, so she thought it sounded like a grand idea and something of an adventure.

The house was very large and spread out. No one had greeted them at the door. They took a quick look through the house but found no one. By the time they finished, dark clouds had appeared on the horizon. It was easy to see a storm was coming. Henrietta refused to accompany her cousin back to town. He'd have to go by himself to retrieve their luggage. She'd complained the automobile had no top, and rain was obviously going to start. She didn't want to get her good skirt soaked. Now she dearly wished she'd gone anyway. In addition to their trunks, all of their other worldly possessions were in crates that rested at the railroad station. Reluctantly, James left her, promising to return as soon as he possibly could.

At first she'd had fun pretending to be the lady of the house. Tiring of that, she tried pretending to be an archaeologist who'd discovered an ancient civilization. That was a good excuse to go snooping. But that had been hours ago. The wind rose, and rain began pouring down shortly after James had left. As it fell, so did the temperature. When the hail began, she became worried. She could have kicked herself. She'd left her coat on the seat of the automobile, and it was now far too cold, wet, and windy to walk anywhere.

She'd searched the house and found it well furnished but completely unoccupied. The locked door off the kitchen led to the pantry, but try as she might, she could not get it open. She could reach a woodpile outside near the kitchen door. Thank goodness James still had not completely given up his nasty habit of smoking. She carried a packet of matches for him in her purse while he carried none. That way, he always had to ask her for a light, and she could scold him. Very unladylike, she whispered, "Damn you anyway. Where are you?"

This was hardly what she expected. She made the trip because of the pleas and promises of her uncle Robert. According to him the journey would bring her to a place where she would be free from want or worry. Finding herself alone in a strange house that lacked food, warmth or company did not fulfill those expectations. Exhausted from the day's activities there was nothing to do but wait for James to return. She settled down in the chair and drifted off to sleep.

It continued to rain and sometimes hail until nearly dawn. Then it started to clear. The morning broke with a few high white clouds and brilliant sunshine. The sky was once again that beautiful blue one sees only in the dead of winter and just after a spring storm. The ground was soaked, but the gravel drive drained well, and by the time the sun was fully up, it looked as if it was going to be a very nice day.

It was still too cool to walk without a coat. Henrietta decided to wait until midday. By then the warm front had done its work, and though slightly brisk, the day wasn't too bad. She headed down the drive. Once she reached the road, she turned left to go down the hill, not up, to her right. What passed for hills in that part of Oklahoma would have been considered flat in any other part of the world. She still didn't know if there was anything to her right except empty space. The road she was on went down to the low water crossing and then back up the hill toward town. It was at least a six- or seven-mile hike.

As Henrietta approached the crossing in the eerie silence, all she could hear was the sound of running water. Her worst fear was realized when she crested the last small rise and saw the swollen creek for herself. The water looked far too deep and cold to permit a crossing. That part of the world was so flat that when it rained hard, the runoff had no place to go, and local flooding was common. Rather than give up, having come that far, she decided to walk up the side of the creek to see if she could find a place to cross. A small tree and some underbrush were a few hundred yards off to her right, so she headed in that direction. She watched where she stepped, trying to stay out of the worst part of the mud. As she got close to the underbrush, she noticed the ground ahead rose slightly, and there was a flattened area.

The closer she got, the more Henrietta could see the area had been disturbed. Mounting the rise, she saw the entire area had been mashed down and was full of tracks. She looked closely. There in the center of the clearing was an oblong section of dirt perhaps six or seven feet long and half that wide. The dirt was piled up in a mound. Next to the long sides of the dirt pile, the ground was very smooth as though it had been covered. She'd seen something like this before. "Oh my," she gasped. "It looks just like...." She gasped again. "It looks just like a freshly closed grave."

It hadn't been there before, or if it had been, she would have noticed it. Having nothing better to do, Henrietta picked her way closer. Something was on the ground next to the grave. There was one woman's shoe print in the mud. It looked as if there might have been a struggle as the ground around the dirt mound was very roughed up and the plants bent down. It didn't make sense. Maybe it was the scene of a murder! Maybe outlaw desperados or rampaging wild Indians had killed some poor woman.

Later, Henrietta would conclude it had just been her imagination playing tricks on her. It had been a long time since she'd been completely alone. The last time involved a deliberate attempt to scare her with a haunted house ghost story. Now, thanks to the dime novels she favored reading, her mind was full of gruesome images. Pictures of evil wild Indians trying to scalp her was one. Then reason took hold. Wild Indians wouldn't take the time to bury a body. She wasn't sure about outlaws, but she thought they wouldn't take the time to bury anyone either—but she wasn't sure. Still, she was convinced she was in mortal danger. She froze and listened. All she could hear was the creek. Slowly she surveyed her surroundings. She was alone. Backing away, her mind raced. She walked quickly, then broke into a run back toward the house. Out of breath, she closed the door behind her and locked it.

Sinking to the floor, Henrietta began to shake. She sat there for several minutes. Had a woman been murdered at the creek? If she had been and whoever had killed her hadn't crossed the creek before the rain, the chances were good the murderer was still nearby.

She cautiously went to the window. Peeking outside, she saw nothing. Then just as quickly as she could, she ducked back down. *I'm being stupid*, she thought to herself. Aloud, she added, "If someone is out there, they've seen me come and go, and the smoke from the fireplace is a dead giveaway. I don't mean a 'dead giveaway.' I mean an 'obvious indication.' No sense in tempting fate." She paused and then said, "Great. Now I'm talking to myself. What's next?" That made her giggle. "I'm being foolish. I'm a full-grown adult, not a child! Adults don't run away like silly schoolgirls."

Henrietta stood up, squared her shoulders, and said, "I'm tired, cold, hungry, and sick of it." She went to the fireplace. The embers were still glowing, so she added several logs. In a few minutes, the heat from the rebuilt fire warmed the room. That helped, and she mused out loud, "At least if I'm going to die, it won't be from freezing to death." It would be at least a day before the creek fell enough to get across. She knew she was facing another long night alone.

She went back into her uncle's study. She searched every drawer and every cupboard. Not finding what she wanted, she went into every room in the house. Try as she might, she could find nothing resembling a gun. The closest thing she found to a proper weapon was a small, dull kitchen knife. Holding it close, she gave up the search. She went back to her chair in front of the fire, sat down, pulled a blanket around her, and all alone, she thought about crying but stopped herself. *Get a grip on yourself, girl! You're made of sterner stuff than fluff. Just because you're alone and hungry, there is nothing to be afraid of!*

Henrietta giggled as she made her way into the library. She began by flipping through a stack of books set aside near one overstuffed chair. All were apocalyptic or post-apocalyptic fiction. On top was Mary Shelly's *The Last Man*. Next was a copy of Richard Jefferies *After London*. Under that was H. G. Well's *War of the Worlds*. Why her uncle was reading about the end of the world she could not imagine. In any event these books were not what she needed; stuck as she was. She needed something to cheer her up. Wandering to the shelves she continued to look. Deciding *Robinson Crusoe* bore too close a resemblance to her plight she settled upon *Joan of Arc* by Mark Twain. Henrietta was familiar with her story but had not read the book. She liked the idea that it might take a young woman to save a country. Book in hand, she settled in for a long day. When darkness fell she continued to read by firelight until the arms of Morpheus enveloped her.

The morning sun came up in a beautiful clear sky. Southern winds overnight had warmed the air, and the sun held the promise that soon it would be very comfortable to be outside without a coat. Henrietta waited until the sun got above the few trees. Screwing up her courage, she again headed down the drive to the road.

She turned left toward the creek. As she crested the rise, she listened. The sound of rushing water was gone. As the creek came into view, she could see it was low enough to cross. She looked to where she'd seen the pile of dirt and the woman's shoe print the day before. "Where is it? I could swear it was right here." It was gone!

Henrietta walked forward, thinking she had just been confused, but as she walked, she could see her own footprints in the mud. They led to where the pile of dirt and the shoeprint had been. She looked more closely. The pile of dirt was still there and next to it the shoeprint. It was definitely from a woman's shoe, but it was not hers. Standing in the silence next to what she had thought might be a fresh grave was downright creepy. She listened closely. She heard the water and a few birds but nothing at all that sounded human, just the water, wind, and wild. This was very creepy.

Henrietta walked back to the crossing. She took off her boots and stockings. She rolled up the legs to her knickers and gathered her skirt and petticoat. Taking a deep breath and bracing herself, she stepped into the water. It wasn't nearly as deep as she'd feared. It was cold, but she could take it. She crossed to the far side.

She sat down on a rocky area in the sun. The sun was far up into the sky, and it had already warmed up nicely. She didn't want to put her boots on wet. That would only make the long walk more uncomfortable. As it was, fashionable pointed-toe boots with two-and-a-half-inch heels were hardly ideal for hiking. She thought about taking her skirt off to dry her feet but reconsidered. "No, someone might come along. I'll just wait." The slight breeze was warm. That and the sunshine dried her feet and legs. After a time, she put her stockings and boots on and started toward town. It was going to be a long walk, and she was hardly dressed for it. The high-collared white cotton blouse, long navy blue skirt, and custom-made high heel boots were far better suited for having tea in a sitting room or riding in an automobile than hiking cross country. Henrietta's hat was another matter altogether. Its wide brim and dark blue band made it very fashionable, but even with a scarf under her chin, every wind gust threated to take it from her.

The road meandered through the county. The open fields were separated by fencerows and, from time to time, a few heat-stressed trees. As the sun passed its zenith, the temperature became very comfortable, or would have it had not been for the fact that the only sound Henrietta heard was her shoes on the gravel. Just bugs and birds, nothing mechanical, not anything at all. She walked, but her shoes and the uneven gravel made it tough going. It was nearly an hour before she reached the first house. Seeing the end of a drive, she quickened her pace. Reaching the drive, she stopped and looked closely for signs of life. She could see the walkway leading to the front steps, the flower garden, and the swing on the one large tree in the front yard. She remembered this place. It was a charming little house they had passed on their way to her uncle's home. The drive was empty. It was all just as it should have been, except for the fact it was deserted. She walked up the drive and then to the front door and knocked. There was no answer. She peered through the window. The house looked empty. *They must have moved*, she thought and tested the front door. It was locked tight. She gave up and went back down the drive to the road.

It was a good mile to the next house, which sat back from the road. The drive next to the house was empty. Henrietta walked up to the front door and knocked. There was no answer, so she knocked a second time. Again there was no answer. The door was locked and the curtains drawn. She gave up and moved on. The town was only three-quarters of a mile farther on. There was bound to be traffic. There always was traffic in towns. Even here in the wilds of America, there should be someone. She listened. Still nothing.

Macnevin, Oklahoma, wasn't much of a big place anymore. In fact, it never had been much. The railroad ran through town, but any commerce that had been hoped for never materialized. On the edge of town was the old livery stable. Part of it had been converted to service automobiles, or so said the sign out front. James pointed it out to Henrietta when they were in the automobile. He surmised the manager and his wife lived in the house next door and it would always be open. Today it was dark and the door was closed. There were none of the customary sounds of a stable or a garage emanating from the building. On a pretty day like this, the doors should have stood open welcoming customers.

Henrietta put her fingers into the small gap in the center of the doors and pulled. The doors parted just enough so she could slip in. It was dark. "Hello."

She paused. No response. "Hello." Nothing. "Hello! Fine, I'll just help myself." She looked first in one stall then another. All were empty. There were no horses, automobiles, or trucks to be found.

She went back outside and saw the handle for the well. She pumped it several times, and water poured out into a bucket. Cupping her hands, she caught some and took a drink. It was very cold. *Good*, she thought. Then out loud, she said, "Now to find somewhere to get something to eat."

A short way from the livery stable was the train station. It was also deserted, dark, and empty. Where was the station master? Henrietta looked around. The trunks were sitting inside, together with the crates that held their belongings. Nothing had been moved since it had been taken off the train. When the train she and her cousin had arrived on pulled in and stopped for more than water and to drop off mail, it had been an event. A few people came out to take a look. Now there was no one…nor were there any automobiles or trucks on the streets.

Up to that point, she'd tried to convince herself it was all nothing more than an elaborate game, but this was going too far. What kind of disaster could have occurred that took everyone away? She couldn't imagine anything natural. Well past scared, her mind began to fill with images of man-made disasters. Could some terrible accident have happened? Or worse yet, could this be deliberate depopulation as might happen in a war? Once her imagination took over there was no stopping it. In only moments she was shaking with fear. After a few long minutes she began to get a grip on herself. *There must be a logical reason for all of this and absolutely no purpose will be served by panicking.* Now mad at herself she became indignant! Who could be behind such a stunt? She ran from store to store. There were only four left on Main Street that faced the railroad tracks. Each was closed and locked. The one restaurant was also closed.

Henrietta began yelling. "Hello! Is there anyone here? Hello! Where is everyone? Hello! Help! Help me, please! Hello! Somebody answer me! Hello!"

No one answered. In a most ungentle way, she whispered, "Damn. Damn. Damn!" She looked around. Where could everyone be? She stared at the empty street. *I need wheels*, she thought.

Henrietta returned to the station and found her trunk. Everything was as she remembered it. She removed a riding skirt, cloth coat, and pair of gloves. Digging in the second drawer, she found the pistol James had given her when he told her they would be moving to the wilds of "no man's land in the Cimarron Territory of the Americas." He'd considered it a joke, but she hadn't.

She was already a good shot thanks to her father's fascination with firearms. James had teased her saying, "I know you're a lady now, but at least you could wave it at someone if you had to."

"I'll have you know I'm a crack shot," she'd replied indignantly.

"Shooting a paper target is one thing..."

"I know. Even so, I could shoot someone if I had to. After all, I had to put down Toby when he broke his leg. I loved that horse."

"What? You shot a horse?"

"My horse. It was my fault he broke his leg. It was my duty."

"When did this happen?"

"When I was sixteen. Toby was mine. I raised him, and...I'd been warned not to, and, well, I was stupid and showing off, and I jumped him anyway, and he broke his leg."

"They made you shoot him?"

"No, I took the gun and did it myself. I had to, you see. I was responsible." She paused, then explained, "My father used to tell me that when you take on a responsibility, you must see it through. I was the one who thought she knew better. I didn't mean to hurt my horse, but I did. Someone had to kill the poor animal. I hope to heaven I never have to shoot another living thing, but I had to do it because...I started it, and that made me responsible. I had to see it through...to the end."

With this in mind, Henrietta faithfully practiced with the pistol until she was satisfied she could hit what she aimed at. Having found the treasured Colt 1903 hammerless semi-automatic 32 caliber pistol, she slipped it into the pocket of her coat and began opening one of the crates. She was still very much on her own, but now she'd have a fighting chance if there was trouble.

The crate held one of her greatest treasures—a lady's bicycle manufactured in Wolverhampton, England. It was beautiful and boasted a fully enclosed chain drive. It also had guard strings running from the rear fender to the axle. The clever design prevented her riding skirt from ever getting caught in the bicycle's mechanism as she rode.

The front wheel of the bicycle had been removed for shipment. It took Henrietta forty-five minutes to search the other crates before she found her tool kit. With it in hand, she managed to get the wheel back on. She took time to adjust the seat and handlebars as best she could. She also managed to locate her wicker bicycle basket. It was a clever design with a handle and a lid. Two small straps allowed her to attach it to the handlebars. It was just the right thing to bring a book and a bit to eat when she launched off on an outing. She loved the freedom that came from riding on her bicycle, just as much as riding in a car or on a horse. Now it was a perfect solution since there were no automobiles or horses to be had.

Henrietta surveyed her belongings. There was nothing among them she couldn't live without except a small stack of letters tied up with a now faded and worn ribbon. These were the first love letters she'd ever received. They were from a boy she'd not seen in years. Written in the halting hand of the boy, there was something about them that spoke to her. Whenever she was depressed she'd take them out and remember her feelings from long ago. She knew she was being silly. That boy was now a man and who knew how he'd turned out. If they ever saw each other again what could she possibly say to him? Even so, she liked to imagine he'd grown into a man she could love; someone who would sweep her off her feet. It was only a fantasy, but a happy one.

Henrietta smiled as she looked at the letters. Silly or not, the letters acted like a tonic. With whatever was going on she might have need of that tonic. She put the letters in the basket together with the tool kit. She then changed into her riding skirt. Mounting her bicycle, she began a circuit around town in hopes of finding someone. She had no luck. Every house and every business was closed, locked, and appeared unoccupied. Giving up, she mumbled, "Dear Lord, what has happened? Is this the end of the world?" Then with a smile she added, "If it is the end of the world, I might as well go into the light doing something I enjoy. I'll go shopping." She peddled back to the grocery store.

The door was still locked. Now equipped with her tool kit, Henrietta made short work of the lock and managed to trip the latch. Inside, the only light was from the front windows. The shelves were empty. Now truly confused, she slowly made her way back to the station and picked up a few items of clothing from her trunk. Putting some items on over her clothes and other bits in the basket, she looked like a ragpicker. It didn't matter; no one would see her. The sky had begun to look dark and menacing.

As she rode through the countryside, Henrietta remembered some of the dime novels her mommy had so disapproved of. They were western adventures, and she loved them. She imagined herself as a lonely cowpoke heroine riding the range in search of her lost love, ready at a moment's notice to take on a band of outlaws or desperados. It was all very romantic but awfully silly. If she'd been a real cowpoke, she'd have been on a horse, not an English-made bicycle in a skirt!

When she coasted down a slight grade, Henrietta moved on to pretending she was flying. She laughed out loud. It was fun, and it passed the time. By the time she got to the house, she was tired.

Chapter Two:
Company Arrives

The sky had given fair warning, and it began to rain again. The fire was nearly out, so Henrietta rebuilt it first. Then, using her trusty bicycle tools, she got the pantry door open.

To her delight, the pantry was full. Eyeing all that she found, she started planning a meal. After locating the pots and pans she'd need, she tried to figure out how to use the oven and cook stove without burning the house down. It wasn't too much different from the ones she's seen before. Despite repeated attempts, she failed to get the gas on or the pilot lights lit. Giving up, she mumbled, "I guess I'm camping out again tonight." She sighed heavily.

She pulled a cast iron Dutch oven out of the pantry and, using a technique she'd learned from one of the western adventure books she'd read, she made cowboy biscuits. Tasting one, she grimaced and said, "They're not too bad… if you're starving." Henrietta also found several cans of soup and a ham. She would heat the soup then finish the meal with several cookies. It wasn't the fine dining she was accustomed to, but it was to be her first proper meal in two days.

The storm had built and was coming through. It wasn't as big as the earlier storm, but it was enough. She decided going out anymore was out of the question. *It is time to have something to eat, take a hot bath, then go to bed*, she thought.

Before starting dinner, Henrietta realized her wood supply inside was dwindling. She examined the heaters but hadn't been able to get any of them lit. It didn't matter. The wood pile was only a short distance from the kitchen door. She waited until the rain let up a little and then ran to pick up the logs she needed. They were soaking wet. She put a couple on the fire, which began to smoke badly. Surveying the situation, she decided to go and get more wood. She'd calculated that if she let the wood dry before she put it on the fire, it would work better. She went out several times. Each time, she considered cursing the fact she was getting soaked by the cold rain. As she prepared to heat up the soup, she decided she should get one more load of wood to make it through the night.

She actually made three trips to the woodpile. On her third trip, it was already nearly pitch dark and very difficult to see. Suddenly she stopped and stood frozen. What was she hearing? After days with only birds, bugs, and wind, the sound of a steam engine was unmistakable. She listened. It was an engine, and it was headed her way.

Henrietta dropped the wood and ran back into the house. She pulled off her wet coat and then, gun in hand, went to the door but did not open it. The automobile was on the drive. Its headlights were on and it had its top up, so she couldn't see the occupant clearly. The driver's side door opened, and a figure emerged. It looked like a man. He closed the door and ran to the front porch. Underneath its shelter, he said, "Hello in the house. Is anyone here?" Then he waited.

Henrietta took a deep breath. "Yes, what do you want?"

"Thank God there is someone else! I thought I was completely alone!"

"What?"

"You're the first person I've talked to in three days. Are you alone? Can I come in?"

He was the first person Henrietta had talked to in what seemed like weeks but had been only days. It was night, and they were alone. What would he do if she refused? Eventually she'd concluded that at some point she'd have to deal with him. "I have a gun, so no sudden moves. The door is unlocked. Come in slowly."

She stepped back. The door opened slowly. The man who stood before her was tall and good looking with blonde hair and piercing blue eyes. He clearly needed a shave and a bath. "Who are you?" she demanded.

"I'm Alexander. That's Alexander VonKleist. Who are you?"

With a very proper English accent, Henrietta replied, "I'm Lady Henrietta Turnbull."

She'd decided to use her uncle's last name rather than her real name of Whitfield. She reasoned its familiarity would carry more weight in these regions than would an unknown one. She could only imagine what Americans might make of her claiming to be Lady Whitfield. This was particularly true given her experience while on the ship. She'd made the mistake of making reference to her father's title. He was Edward Whitfield and officially the 6th Earl of Hardingham. That title had caused her no little amount of embarrassment thanks to a comedic offering on the London and New York stages featuring a buffoon pirate king. Wags had christened her with an unflattering moniker more befitting the daughter of a buccaneer than an English lady. So rather than again be that "wild pirate's daughter," or something worse, she'd settled on the deceit of simply being a Turnbull.

Henrietta asked, "Do you have any idea what is going on? With everyone gone I started to get worried that something terrible happened."

"Terrible? Like what."

Well I don't know exactly. Perhaps a natural disaster or maybe something worse. When I was still in Britain the newspapers were full of news that a war was imminent. I didn't believe it because that is always the news, but still I thought maybe a war had started…"

"No, no, nothing like that is going on. There isn't a war; not at all. It was just a big storm; not a war."

The insistence of Alexander's answer left Henrietta uncertain, but she remained silent. Alexander paused for a moment then continued: "I was out in it, and my automobile was wrecked by the wind. I had to fix it. Then I headed over this way looking for help. I was coming here when I smelled the smoke from your chimney."

"Smoke? How? I'm well off the main road."

"When I came down the road looking for this place, I smelled your smoke."

"You could really smell it?"

"When you burn wet wood, sometimes it smokes pretty badly."

"Yes, I discovered that."

"So I smelled it. That's all."

"So where were you headed?"

"As I said, I was trying to find the home of my employer, Robert Turnbull."

"Uncle Robert employs you?"

Alexander nodded.

They stood and looked at each other for a few moments. Then Henrietta said, "I am his niece. May I ask in what capacity my uncle Robert employs you?"

Alexander blinked. "Excuse me, your…ladyship? I…I am an engineer, and he hired me for a special project, but I have been instructed not to speak about it."

Henrietta considered for a moment and then said, "Very well, if you can't or won't say—"

Alexander interrupted her. "Please, ma'am, I know I look pretty rough, but it's been a hard couple of days, and…well, you don't need to worry about me. I figure you and I…I work for your uncle. The last thing I want…that we need…is for you to be afraid I'll try something. I mean it. I'm tired and sick of being alone, and I think you are too. So as I said, please don't worry. I won't try anything, not anything at all. I promise."

Henrietta eyed him cautiously. He seemed so sincere, and he was right; she was scared. Just to have someone to talk to was a blessing. "OK, please come in," she said and lowered the gun.

He smiled. "Do you have anything to eat? I haven't had anything since yesterday."

"Yes, I was about to make dinner for myself. Would you like to join me?"

"Dinner! Yes, certainly. You are an angel who has come in answer to my prayers."

"No, I…look, let's get you something to eat and then cleaned up. After that, we can talk."

"Thank you. What can I do?"

"Well, do you have anything in your vehicle we might be able to use?"

"Yeah, a few things."

"You start bringing it in, and I will get back in the kitchen and finish the preparations."

"Fair enough."

Henrietta went back into the kitchen. She pulled out two more cans of soup and some canned fruit. Now that she'd tried to make biscuits once, she knew what she'd done wrong. This second batch would be much better. Thank heavens her governess, Mrs. Peabody, had taught her how to cook when she was growing up. Henrietta was very proud of her skill in the kitchen and had joked with her cousin that if they ever were forced to live on their own, she could make her own way hiring on as a cook. It didn't take her long to finish the biscuits. Once they were on the fire, she stood back and admired her work.

Alexander came back in. "I have more," he said. He made several more trips.

In between loads, Henrietta told him, "I have biscuits cooking. They should be ready in just a few minutes."

As soon as they were ready, she gave him two with butter and jelly. He inhaled the biscuits. "Thank you, ma'am. You cannot imagine how good that tasted. All I've had for the last couple of days was a bite of hard candy and a little beef jerky."

"You are more than welcome. Now, before we sit down and have dinner and talk, I have a bucket of water for your bath heating on the fire."

"A bath with real soap and everything?"

"Yes. And I found some of my Uncle Robert's clean clothes. You can wear them while yours dry."

"Your Uncle Robert won't mind?"

"No, I don't think so…not under the circumstances. Pity I didn't think to get anything from my cousin's trunk."

"Your cousin?"

"Yes. He dropped me off here, and I haven't seen him since. His trunk is still at the train station in town."

It started to rain heavily outside, and thunder in the distance shook the house. Alexander asked, "So what about you?"

"Well, I've been here mostly, but, well…I really would prefer it if you got cleaned up first. Then we'll be able to enjoy our dinner and talk."

"That sounds like a very good plan. I guess I am a bit ripe." Henrietta was too much of a lady to do anything but nod. Alexander looked down and said, "If that water is close, a bath really does sound great."

"It's almost there if it's not already. Why not go half-fill the tub, and I'll bring the hot water to you?"

Alexander went into the bathroom, and a few minutes later, Henrietta tapped on the door. "Water's ready."

"I'm not decent. Leave it in the hall, and I'll get it."

"OK," she said and put the bucket down. "I'll wait for the bucket and start a second one if this isn't enough." She turned away, and he reached out and grabbed the bucket. She heard the water splash.

"Bucket coming out." The door opened, and Alexander put the bucket on the floor. "Thank you."

On hearing that, Henrietta picked up the bucket, and the process was repeated. "I've laid out some of my Uncle Robert's clothes in the bedroom. Please join me in the dining room when you are dressed."

She waited and was soon rewarded with the company of a newly scrubbed, handsome young man. Her uncle's clothes suited him nicely.

"Thank you again for taking me in," he began.

Henrietta smiled. "So tell me.... What has happened, and how did you end up here?"

"Well, I work for your uncle and was helping with clearing the area. I stopped for the night and was staying in this farmhouse. The storm got pretty bad, so I hid in the storm cellar. The next morning, when I woke up, my car had been wrecked. I had to work a long time to get it running again, but I finally managed to fix it. Then I remembered Mr. Turnbull lived over this way. That's why I came here."

Outside, the rain was falling hard. Alexander told Henrietta about growing up in a small town in Illinois and then going to the engineering school at the University of Michigan, where he played football, and then how he'd gone on to attend the Massachusetts Institute of Technology. He'd worked in Europe for a time, and then he'd been hired by her uncle to work on the Project.

In turn, Henrietta found herself having to make up all sort of things to tell him. Rightfully, she was an English lady, just as she had earlier suggested. However, she was the American tomboy daughter of an English father and mother. The marriage of Edward Whitfield to Beatrice Turnbull had been something of a scandal, and the couple had run off to America. Henrietta was born in New York. Edward's father, the earl, insisted his son return to England or be cut off completely. He refused. Her father and mother remained in America living under a false name.

Making it on his own was beyond her father's ability, so both he and his wife worked. By the time Henrietta was three, her parents were so busy, she'd been left with a woman in the neighborhood to raise her. Mrs. Peabody was a kind, gentle soul, whom her father made a home for in exchange for looking after the child. Inwardly, Mrs. Peabody was a woman who believed she'd been cheated by life. Her late husband had worked as a scientist and instructor at a private college, and she had been his assistant, though she had had no formal education past high school. He had been well respected but hardly rich. Without children, their life had been comfortable. When he had fallen ill, they spent what savings they had in a vain attempt to save him. He died leaving her penniless and deeply in debt. The college paid her husband's bills but otherwise abandoned her. They had no place for a mere woman who had no degree. She cast about for some way to make a living, but many doors were closed because she lacked formal education and many others because she was just a woman.

The offer from Henrietta's father had come as a godsend. As Henrietta's parents' financial circumstances improved, Mrs. Peabody stayed on and effectively became her governess. She filled Henrietta with her ideas about the role of women in society. She believed women were equal to men and many times their superior. She was an ardent suffragette. She encouraged Henrietta, telling her repeatedly, "A woman must be more than a pretty face, ribbons, and lace. You must make something of yourself, or you will end up like me, having to depend on men." Henrietta enjoyed "playing dress-up" but understood if she wanted to be her own person, she needed to learn how to be more like the men she admired. She was an unabashed tomboy. She loved to climb trees and play baseball. She could throw, catch, and hit with the best of the boys.

Unaware of his daughter's indoctrination, Henrietta's father responded poorly whenever his daughter acted "unladylike" or challenged his authority. He would say, "Henrietta, you may be cleverer than other girls, and you may possess many interests not usually associated women, but you are still a young lady and must act like one!"

When she turned twelve, her father's circumstances changed dramatically, and the family moved back to England. Henrietta refused to go without Mrs. Peabody. As a compromise, Henrietta's father created a trust fund for the soon-to-be unemployed governess. As a condition, Mrs. Peabody agreed to move to California. There she would find love and a new life.

Henrietta's father told his daughter he wanted her to move to Britain so she could, "pick up some of the good habits a lady needs if you ever want to be more than a trollop or a trolley maid." Father Edward was now an earl and her mother, Beatrice, was a countess.

Her mother's path to becoming a countess was unusual. Beatrice's father was something of an eccentric visionary and had encouraged his daughter to pursue an education along with her brothers. While attending university in London, she had met and married the youngest son of an earl. The boy was smart but undisciplined. He was considered a black sheep and had a reputation as a rebellious hellion. They'd married and run off to America. All that changed when Henrietta's grandfather and then three of her father's older brothers all unexpected died. The title fell to Edward when Henrietta was nearly thirteen.

Edward and Beatrice had only the one daughter. Henrietta was not the son he'd hoped for, but her strong, independent character made up for it. Having gone to an all-boys school and never having had a daughter, her father knew nothing of how to raise a girl. He treated her like one of the boys, much to his wife's distress. Henrietta, by the time she started at university, could ride and shoot with the best of them. She played a fair game of cricket and could drink whisky neat. Her skills were not limited to acting manly. Henrietta possessed a good ear for music and quickly mastered the peculiarities of a refined English accent. Thanks to diction and deportment lessons provided by her mother, she very soon could pass easily for a child born and raised her whole life in a large country house in Britain.

Her mother, Beatrice, asked Henrietta to begin calling her "Mother" rather than the sour and icy "Mommy" she'd adopted since arriving "back home." Mrs. Peabody had been more of a mother to her than her real mother, so Henrietta always referred to Beatrice as "Mommy" or "Mommy dearest" just to annoy her. Henrietta liked her father and had a wide range of names she affectionately used with him, including "Father," "Daddy," and "Pops."

To be proper, one would address "Mommy" as Lady Hardingham. She lavished attention on her daughter, the newly minted Lady Henrietta. She did her very best to transform the child from an adventurous, headstrong young American tomboy into a refined and accomplished young lady of good breeding. In addition to being very pretty, Henrietta was smart, quick, and exceptionally clever. She could boast of a remarkable gift for mathematics. But her inquisitive nature led her to study subjects as varied as astronomy, military history, and stage magic. Henrietta understood what was expected of her now but considered her new outward appearance and mannerisms a mere façade hiding the same little American girl who still longed for adventure. She chafed under the restrictions common to her new status and station.

Everything was going well and Henrietta's prospects looked very promising, but she turned down several proposals, choosing to pursue her education before becoming tied down in a marriage. It was all going according to plan until her father lost most of the family's fortune. He proved ill-prepared to oversee the estate, and it proved too much for him. Through a series of ill-advised and speculative investments, he'd frittered his birthright away. In the end, thanks to Uncle Robert, this was of little consequence to Henrietta. It was her intention to finish her education and then begin a life of adventure. One of her persistent dreams was to become involved with the new science of flight. She imagined that one day she might follow in the footsteps of the Brazilian Alberto Santos-Dumont, who flew his dirigible seven whole miles from Saint-Cloud in Paris to the Eiffel Tower and won the 100,000-franc Deutsch Prize. Even more, she imagined meeting Germany's own Count Zeppelin. He built and flew the most amazing airships in the world.

Henrietta's imagination knew no boundaries. She hoped that one day, she herself might explore the world by air. Even so, she was a realist and appreciated the limitations of current airships. If she wanted to explore a more conventional mode of transport would be required. To that end, she had studied mathematics and engineering. With the help of a kind neighbor, a retired Royal Navy captain who had inherited a title and left active service after he lost his leg fighting pirates off the China coast, she used her gift for mathematics to master the intricacies of navigation. Believing what Mrs. Peabody taught her, that a woman was the equal of a man, Henrietta reasoned she should join the Royal Navy. As a captain of a ship she could lead voyages of adventure. The Royal Navy did not share her belief and politely turned down her application. Not deterred, Henrietta continued her studies and mastered all the requirements necessary to pass the examination to become a lieutenant. Several more applications, accompanied by recommendations from a dozen retired senior officer attesting to her qualification were submitted. Each was supposedly reviewed but all were rejected. The Royal Navy was not prepared to accept a woman no matter who she was. Henrietta's only paused her efforts when the earl, her dear papa, fell from his horse while fox hunting and struck his head. It left him a crippled shell of a man and in agony. He lingered on for more than a year, and when he finally died, it was a relief.

That he was gone was bad enough, but with his death, his financial losses became known. The now nearly worthless title passed to a rather pompous male cousin named William, with whom Henrietta and her mother had a falling out. William had made his own fortune from the shipping trades and used part of it to recover the ancestral home from creditors. He assigned Beatrice and Henrietta blame for the condition of the estate, although they had had nothing to do with it. Then he threw them out to fend for themselves. Beatrice and Henrietta were destitute and were forced to live off the generosity of others.

Uncle Robert was a genius, willing to embrace new and innovative technologies. It had netted him a significant fortune. He married the love of his life, Charlotte Danvers, but she had died in childbirth. His second marriage, to Abigayle Danforth, was not a happy one and ended when she died in a disastrous train derailment. It had been so unhappy an affair that Uncle Robert never took another wife and was left childless. He threw himself tirelessly into his work.

Now one of the richest men in the land, he found himself in need of an heir. When his brother-in-law died, Uncle Robert resolved to become Henrietta's salvation. He offered Beatrice and Henrietta a home, albeit one in the middle of the Oklahoma wilderness. At Beatrice's suggestion, Robert had even offered Henrietta's cousin James, whom both Beatrice and Henrietta liked, an exciting job in his newest enterprise. The two youngsters had remained close and decided to take Uncle Robert up on his offer. Beatrice declined, but even so, Robert, as her younger brother, kindly sent his sister funds and asked her to move into a house he owned. Beatrice would remain in Britain and live comfortably, in the same style she had become accustomed to as the wife of an English earl.

Using her acquired accent, Henrietta now spoke of her sea voyage as though she had traveled across the ocean in luxury and the train trip out to the territory had been in a private railcar. Truthfully, she hadn't sailed first class on a luxury liner but rather on a much smaller tramp steamer. The train trip to the West had been on second- and sometimes third-class tickets. Most of the money her uncle Robert had sent for the passage had been needed to satisfy one of her papa's accounts before they left Britain. She and her cousin could simply not bring themselves to ask for more of a handout. Lastly, she told Alexander of her cousin and the car disappearing.

He sat and listened with rapt attention, enchanted by the sound of Henrietta's voice. At the end, he said, "I could listen to you talk forever, but it is getting late. I do need some sleep. I suppose as a single woman, a lady alone, you would prefer if I slept in the barn with the car tonight."

"Don't be silly. There are plenty of empty beds in the house. You are certainly welcome to one of them." Then with a smile she added, "That is, if your engineering training includes how to make these American gas heaters work."

Alexander said with a grin, "It does. I can show you how. It is fairly easy if you know where the cutoff valve is."

"I didn't know..."

"That's all right. Out here in this part of the world, you have a lot of heat in the summer, so in some houses, there is a way to cut the gas off to the heaters when you are away. That way, they can put the pilot light out and not have to worry about an accidental fire. They won't have hidden it. I'll bet it's just outside. Let me take a quick look." It took him only moments to find the valve. "Do you have a pair of pliers?"

She did, and within half an hour, the house began to warm properly. Henrietta made herself at home in the room her uncle Robert had gone to the trouble of setting up for her, and she asked Alexander to stay in the room intended for her cousin.

After a good night's sleep in a proper bed, Henrietta felt wonderful. She got up, dressed, and made her way to the kitchen. Alexander was still sleeping. It appeared he hadn't had a very easy time of it and needed the rest. She busied herself by making breakfast.

When the smells aroused him, Alexander got up, dressed, and joined Henrietta in the kitchen. Unthinkingly, and in her original plain midwestern American accent, she said, "Good morning, Alexander."

"Good morning to you, Lady Henrietta," came the reply.

Henrietta pulled up short, realizing she'd dropped her English accent, so she covered it by saying, "I do so hope I said that correctly? My uncle Robert suggested in his letters that I should learn to speak like an American so as not to draw attention to myself."

Chapter Three:
The Project

Uncle Robert had actually suggested that Henrietta sound as English as possible. For years, he'd privately claimed he was rightfully an English noble; however, his father's title had been a knighthood for military service and did not pass to his heirs. Nonetheless, Robert insisted he was rightfully an English lord and lived in the United States only because he'd opposed the crown's policy in Ireland. It was an unlikely story, but it gave him a certain air of mystery to those who knew no better. He'd tell the story, then add, "But don't call me Sir Robert. It might get back to my enemies. Here in the United States, I am simply Mr. Robert Turnbull."

As a consequence of his experiences, Robert had concluded that a proper English lady might find it easier to gain the protection of anyone who considered himself a gentleman. It was true. Even though Americans eschewed ranks of title for themselves, they appreciated the English practice and responded accordingly. This was particularly true if one dressed and acted the part. Henrietta decided since she was stuck in the wilderness and in desperate need of assistance, there was no alternative but to take advantage of any small benefit her accent might confer.

She smiled and added, "Did you sleep well?"

"Very well, thank you...my lady."

Alexander seemed as if he didn't really have much experience with proper English ladies, so Henrietta decided to relax. She said, "Alexander, since I am working as your cook and have served as your maid, I think we might dispense with my title. After all, we are alone, and this is America."

"Yes, ma'am."

"Please call me by my given name, Henrietta. Should anyone show up and ask how it is we came to be alone in this house, we will explain you are my first cousin."

"Yes, ma'am…I mean yes, Henrietta. I think I would like that."

"Then it is time we ate."

With the gas turned on, the stove and oven worked properly. Henrietta made a feast with what she had on hand. It included eggs, fried bacon, and sausages alongside freshly made skillet cakes, butter, and a tin of syrup. Henrietta apologized. "I'm sorry. It was the best I could do with the limited pantry."

Alexander disagreed, saying, "It's fabulous!" He stuffed himself full. If the meal had any shortcoming, it was only that there was far too much food for just two individuals. He washed it all down with several cups of properly brewed tea.

Henrietta tried again to find out about the Project. She began, "Now that I have bribed you with a bath, a bed, and two proper meals, I was hoping you would tell me about my uncle's project."

Alexander hesitated, then said, "Since you are his niece and have been so kind, I can't see the harm. Your uncle is a genius and has made a truly magical discovery. He's discovered a natural well that spews a kind of gas that is inert and will not burn. It is going to revolutionize the world."

"I don't understand. What kind of gas won't burn?"

"It's helium gas. I've verified it myself. It was thought to be very rare, but your uncle has discovered that it is not."

"And how will this revolutionize the world?"

"I am sure you are aware that several inventors have built rigid airships. In Europe, some even offer passenger service. The problem is, the ships are very dangerous to fly in because hydrogen gas is used to inflate them. Several have burned."

Feigning ignorance in the hope she could learn more, Henrietta said, "And…?"

"The leading authority is Count Zeppelin in Germany. His ships are truly amazing and the very best. His are some of the ones that carry passengers. The latest reports are that he's building a whole fleet. It hasn't become popular because from time to time, even his airships catch fire and crash."

Henrietta blanched. "That's terrible!"

"It is. That is why your uncle's discovery is so revolutionary. He plans to capture the gas and use it in a new fireproof airship. He's planning on building a large commercial ship capable of flying safely anywhere in the world."

"You mean like across the ocean?"

"Absolutely. It will end the monopoly the steamship owners have on overseas travel. One of the railroad barons and an East Coast banker have made significant loans just for that reason. Airships will never carry much freight overland but will give them control of first-class travel. They think they can make a lot of money flying the wealthy around. Best of all, it will put the steamship companies to shame."

Henrietta smiled. Airships that could travel the world. What could possibly be better? Moreover, why would you keep such a marvelous discovery secret? It was all very strange. Past that, if it was secret how did this young man know so much about it? She asked, "If this is all so secret, how is it you know about it?"

"I'm part of your uncle's...well, I guess you might call it his team. He hired me to do a particular job, and my part hasn't really begun, so I got bored just waiting. Some of the others were shorthanded out chasing around in the field, so I thought I'd just volunteer and help them."

"This explains a lot. Uncle Robert asked my cousin James to come and work with him on a secret project. My cousin was working with natural gas."

Alexander continued, "There is more to the story than just that. Your uncle and his partners want to control the gas field here in the strip. The survey team thinks the gas field stretches from Texas all the way across the Cimarron Strip and up to Kansas."

"That is a very large area, isn't it?"

"Maybe a million acres, but that's not so much out here in the West. The entire field is much larger and extends both north and south, but...there are legal problems trying to get a hold of all that land because of the oil companies.

"Is that lawful?"

"Well, I am told it is, at least here in the strip. That's why I was helping make sure there were no other claimants to the land. There are a few folks who have tried to homestead, but they don't really have title to own the land; they're squatters."

"So you have been chasing them off?"

"Oh, no. We've been out buying them out one by one. Your uncle doesn't want anyone to feel they were cheated. That way, the company men will have a clear conscience when they claim title to all of the mineral rights."

"And that is what you were doing when you ended up alone?"

"Yes, and making sure no one was within ten or fifteen miles of the Project."

"Do you know where the Project is?"

"Yes and no."

"What do you mean?"

"I mean, I know the area we were to clear and keep people out of, but I just don't know exactly where the road to the Project is. I've always come and gone from the south and the west. I got pretty turned around with all the clouds and rain and, well, truth is, I'm a little bit lost."

Alexander got up and looked out the window. "It's still raining."

"At least we're dry, and it will give us some time to take inventory of what we have," said Henrietta.

"That's something, at least."

They had another cup of tea. "Let me show you what all I've found," Alexander began.

There was a toolbox and two cardboard boxes full of all sorts of interesting bits and pieces. Henrietta began fingering through them. "Someone was a pack rat," she mused aloud.

"Yes, I guess so. But still, some of it might be useful." Alexander also had some rope and a coil of wire.

Henrietta began thinking about things that seemed out of place. She said, "You know, I think I found a new grave down by the creek."

"Really? How could you tell?"

"It was all disturbed except right where there was a rectangular pile of dirt. It looked as if they'd put boards down next to it for the mourners."

"I bet it wasn't a grave."

"Then what was it?"

"I'll bet if it was close to water, it was a test well. Your uncle had them sunk all over." Still looking out the window, Alexander said, "When it stops raining, I thought I'd go into town."

"I'd like to go with you," said Henrietta. "My trunk is there, and so is my cousin's. I don't know if there is any way, but I'd like to bring as many of our things here as I can."

"I'll be glad to help." Then Alexander turned and started to clear the table, saying, "Since you were kind enough to cook, I'll clear up." Picking up the dishes, he carried them into the kitchen.

Henrietta followed him in. "I'll dry if you wash."

He replied with a smile, "If you'll sit and watch, I'll do both. I'd be glad for the company if you would."

By the time everything was washed, dried, and put away, the sun had come out, and the day had turned nice. Alexander went out and checked the water level in the automobile and then fired up the boiler. In ten minutes, they were on their way.

The vehicle was a large touring car. Alexander saw Henrietta's face when she got her first good look at it in the light. "I know it has seen better days and appears to be held together with wire and prayer. Don't worry; when I fix something, it stays fixed." He was justifiably proud he'd actually managed to get the automobile to run at all. The truth was, it ran a little rough.

Henrietta asked, "What was wrong with the vehicle that kept it from running?"

"The wind got it and flipped it. It bent the axle and tore up the engine. I had to pull it all apart and clear the water line. Then I had to bypass part of the steam generation coil. It cost me about thirty percent of the power the engine used to produce, but we still have plenty to get around. On top of that, I had to build a fire, bend the axle back into shape, and then use brute force to get it all put back together. As you can see, I didn't do much with the fenders except push them out of the way.

Even with the shabby appearance and reduced top speed, the drive to town was exhilarating. Alexander insisted that before loading the trunks on the back rack, he have a chance to look in the livery and garage. He hoped there might be some parts he could use to make his repairs more permanent. When he emerged from the dark building empty-handed, he said, "It appears whoever cleared this place out did a good job. There's nothing inside there but some old horseshoes."

They drove on to the station. Henrietta's trunk was of the large wardrobe variety. It was only with her help that Alexander managed to hoist it up and secure it to the luggage rack. He then loaded her cousin's smaller trunk in the rear seat of the automobile while Henrietta recovered various items from the crates.

She didn't need much of what was in the crates, but as it represented the only things that were hers, she treasured them. It included her large telescope, two side saddles for fox hunting, and her tennis equipment. Her aunt had made sure she had a complete tea service and silver for entertaining. There was a large crate full of books including her copies of the accounts of famous voyages of discovery. Another crate contained her antique sexton and her prized set of navigation charts and maps. She liked to imagine that one day she could use all of it to sail around the world on her own voyages of discovery. For now, most of her belongings would have to remain in the crates at the station.

As they started out from the station in the shabby automobile, fully laden and looking like traveling peddlers or gypsies, the last thing that either of them expected occurred. A man stepped out into the street no more than a hundred yards in front of them. They both stared in amazement as the man waved and started walking toward them.

"Hello. I'm glad I finally found you."

Henrietta and Alexander looked at each other. The man came closer, and Alexander shouted to him, "Is that you, Emmet?"

"Yes. I've been looking for her…that is, if she is Henrietta Whitfield."

Henrietta was nearly dumbfounded but managed to ask, "I am she. And who might you be?"

"I'm Emmet Franklin. Your uncle Robert sent me to collect you."

"I don't understand."

"Your cousin James was in an accident the first day after you arrived. The wind caught him and flipped his automobile. It knocked him out. We found him and took him to safety. He was out cold since. It was only when he finally woke up last night that he told us he'd left you at your uncle's house. I came looking for you. I could see you'd been at the house, and I saw the tire tracks. I figured you'd gotten a ride and come to town. I just followed you here." Turning to Alexander, he asked, "And what happened to you? When you didn't come back, we figured the storm had gotten you too."

"It nearly did. You see what it did to my automobile. I got it working only yesterday and found my way to her."

"Well then, Robert will be glad to see the both of you."

Feeling much better about the situation, Henrietta asked, "So where is my uncle?"

"He's at the Project, ma'am. My instructions are to bring you to him when I find you."

Alexander asked, "Do you have an automobile?"

"Sure do. I've got it parked just around the corner. Let me go get it. then we can all go together." Emmet trotted off. In a few moments, he returned in a very nice new shiny steamer of his own. Stopping next to Alexander's vehicle, he said, "Miss Henrietta, if you'd like to ride with me rather than in that wreck, I'd be pleased to have you."

Henrietta decided that a lady would not abandon her escort, so she said in her best English accent, "No, thank you, Mr. Franklin. Mr. VonKleist has been kind enough to bring me this far. I will continue with him."

"As you choose, ma'am."

As they started off, Alexander smiled and said, "Lady Henrietta, you didn't have to do that."

She returned his smile and said, "It was my pleasure. And as I said, you should just call me Henrietta."

They bounced along the road back toward Uncle Robert's home. Emmet didn't stop but drove past it on the road to nowhere. About five miles along, there in the middle of nowhere was a building on the horizon. As they drew closer, Henrietta could see it was a very large barnlike structure. She realized it wasn't a single building but two, and they were both enormous. She thought there might have been some damage to the roof of the closest one. From the size of the tiny figures of men standing outside, she guessed it was at least a five-story building.

When they finally got close enough, she recognized one of the figures as her uncle. With relief, she cried out, "Uncle Robert!"

"Ah, Henrietta! I am so glad to see you are all right." Seeing Alexander, he added, "And bless you. You've brought my young baron back with you. We're going to need him any day now."

Henrietta looked quizzically at her uncle and asked, "Young baron?"

"He means me," Alexander whispered.

"What? I don't understand."

"In Germany, it's different from what you were used to in Britain. You see, in Germany, if a man is a baron, then all of the sons, not just the oldest, are barons. Barons are everywhere. It's not a big deal as in England. My father was a baron, so I have a title. It's more for show than anything. It's just a courtesy. Now that I'm an American citizen, I go by Alexander."

"Oh, I do understand. I'm entitled to the honorific by reason of my birth, but I grew up as a child here. And why will he need you?"

Henrietta's uncle Robert began to laugh. "You didn't tell her, did you? He's a very experienced aeronaut and has been with me on the Project since the beginning. He's one of the geniuses behind what we've managed to accomplish. More than that, he is going to captain our airship."

Henrietta began to feel she'd been made to play the fool. "You, sir? A baron and aeronaut, and you neglected to tell…allowed me to wait upon you, and…and…?"

"Oh, I am so sorry!" Alexander said, looking down. "I didn't mean to deceive you. It was just that you were being so kind to me when you thought I was no one. I didn't want to spoil it, and now I have. Please forgive me."

Henrietta's anger subsided. She laughed. "I guess I shouldn't complain. I lied to you as well. I am not Henrietta Turnbull…at least not officially. I am Henrietta, daughter of the late Earl of Hardingham."

"I was wondering about that, but…"

Uncle Robert had always found the title funny, so he could not resist the temptation to laugh and say, "Baron, I'm sure you've heard of her father. He's a pirate."

Poor Alexander was caught in the middle with his friend, mentor, and employer on one side and a scowling young woman on the other. He shrugged, then very gallantly said, "In that case, my lady, I am happy you made your introduction as you did, for I never would have believed you had you claimed you were merely a pirate wench." Even Henrietta had to smile at that.

"So, Uncle Robert, now that all of the formalities are finished, would you please tell me about James?"

"Your cousin is going to be just fine. He got a pretty hard bump on the head and broke his arm, but he is safe now and will recover."

"I am so relieved. May I see him?"

"Soon. The doctor has him resting for now. Perhaps a little later would be best."

"Then tell me, Uncle, what is this place?"

"This, my dear, is the Project. It is where we are building a new airship that will change the world."

"Here? In the wilds of the Cimarron Strip?"

"We've had the parts shipped in by rail from all over. We've kept the Project secret for reasons I'll explain later. For now, please understand it is and must remain secret for just a little longer."

"Secret? But…" Henrietta began.

"Henrietta, the world is on the brink of war. The situation is complicated and very dangerous. I will be glad to explain it to you at some time in the future, but for now just trust me."

This didn't satisfy Henrietta, but she knew when no purpose would be served by arguing so she simply nodded and said: "may I at least see the ship?"

Her uncle smiled: "well, you've come this far. Why not?"

They walked to a small door on the side of one of the enormous buildings. Opening it, Henrietta looked inside. She didn't know what to expect to see, but what she saw was incredible.

Inside the building was an airship that filled the space. Her uncle said, "Isn't she beautiful? This is the *Cimarron*. She is six-hundred-fifty-seven feet stem to stern and one-hundred-six feet in diameter. She'll carry a crew and up to forty passengers. Under full steam, we believe she will make seventy miles an hour, maybe more."

Henrietta whispered as though she were in church, "Uncle Robert, I had no idea!"

"No one does, my dear. This is a secret project."

"How soon…?"

"In the next few days. We got very lucky during the storm. We all stayed up all night holding on. Even so, part of the roof of this building blew off. Fortunately, the airship remained safe and undamaged. If it hadn't, we'd have to wait for the other one, which we are just starting on."

"The other one? You have more than one?"

"No, not yet. They just started building the one next door. This is the only one ready, and we are filling the last of the gas bags now. We plan to pull it out for its maiden flight in a day or two. Now that the baron is back with us"—he turned to Alexander—"and if he will behave himself and not go running off again, he can fly the craft."

"Fly?" asked Henrietta.

"Yes, he will fly it. We plan to complete flight training and testing quickly. Once we are certain all is as it should be, we plan to fly first to Washington, then over New York just to show off. Perhaps all the way to London if we can find our way there."

"To London? Is that difficult?"

"Yes, to fly to Washington or New York, all we need to do is follow the railroad. London is across the ocean, and no railroad goes that far."

Alexander added, "We'll need to find a navigator somewhere. Now, come let me show you the inside of the ship."

Henrietta, Alexander, and Robert walked up the gangway into the ship door on the starboard side. From the entry cabin, they took the passageway to the bridge. They passed the kitchen, the radio room, the captain's cabin, the wardroom, and a cabin with a sign on the door saying, "Off limits." Passing the navigation station, they entered the bridge. Henrietta could see that from there, the captain would be able to see out in every direction except directly astern.

At that point, Uncle Robert deferred to Alexander, who was the expert in the matters of controlling the vessel. He explained, "As you see, our bridge is a little different from what you would find on a steamship. The crewmen flying this ship are all seated. It reduces fatigue and helps keep them alert. The captain or officer of the deck sits in this raised swivel chair in the center. He's able to watch over the three control stations and out through the large glass windows. Directly in front of him is the helmsman, or Helm. Helm controls the lateral movement of the ship and keeps it on course. To his left is the flight dynamics station, or Flight. His job is probably the most demanding. He keeps the ship in the air and stable. He'll do that by controlling the lift gas and water ballast. To the right is the propulsion station, or Props. His job is to communicate with the engine compartments and keep output balanced. Behind center seat to the left is the navigator station, or Navigation. To the right rear are the seats for observers and the other officers when they are on the bridge."

Henrietta was fascinated. "It sounds very complicated."

"It was at first, but we built a…I guess you'd call it a simulator, and we've have been practicing. Every man, both here on the bridge as well as elsewhere in the ship, knows exactly what is expected."

"And you will really be the captain?"

"Yes. I have flown before. That's why your uncle Robert chose me to command."

After seeing the bridge, they walked back to the main lounge. It was a large open room with windows running down each side. "This is the salon. It must serve double duty as both our main dining area and primary observation lounge."

At the far end of the salon was a passageway. Uncle Robert led the way. "Back here are the staterooms. We've been very clever in the way we've designed them. Each stateroom is identical, so we need to look at only one."

Henrietta looked inside. Down one side was a couch and on the other bunk beds. On the far wall was a big widow. Uncle Robert said, "This is the clever part." With a flick of a couple of latches, he lowered the top bunk and made the bunk beds into seating couches facing each other. He explained, "This way, we have four bunks to a cabin, giving us room for a total of forty passengers. At the end of the hall, we have two complete lavatory washrooms. At the very end of the hall is a second observation deck that we have designated the smoking lounge. I have otherwise forbidden that nasty habit aboard this ship."

Henrietta was impressed but still had questions. "Uncle Robert, where does the crew sleep?"

"Oh, I guess I didn't point it out, but there are ship's ladders forward and aft. They give access to inside the ship. There are bunks for the crew and storerooms. There is also a gangway that allows us to get to the holds and the engines in flight."

"Show me."

Uncle Robert walked Henrietta into the smoking lounge and pointed to the stairs. "Here is one of them." Henrietta didn't pause to ask permission. Grabbing the rails on each side, she mounted the stairs and disappeared above before her uncle Robert or Alexander could stop her.

It was dark, but not so dark she couldn't see. Forward, she could see the bunks off the gangway, which was wide enough for two people to walk on side by side. Perhaps fifty feet in from the bridge, there was some sort of machinery that obscured the passageway forward. To the rear, there was light from a small window in what appeared to be a door. She immediately started in that direction.

Uncle Robert came up behind Henrietta. "Well, since you're here, I might as well finish the tour." They walked to the doorway.

"Where does that go?"

"Into the forward engine compartment."

Henrietta pushed through. Inside were two large engines with large boilers. Grinning, Uncle Robert said, "We are very proud of these. They are the first of their kind."

"How so?"

"These are special geared turbine steam engines. They are very lightweight and made out of aluminum. Each one produces an unbelievable five hundred horsepower." Henrietta looked skeptical. Uncle Robert continued, "Oh, there are a few steel parts, but to save weight, we've used aluminum for most everything."

By that time, Alexander had joined them. He added, "They're still too heavy. Each one full of water weighs four thousand pounds. They are the heaviest part of the entire ship and cause most of my headaches. They have to be watched constantly."

"It's not that bad," said Uncle Robert. "It's just that we've had problems with some of the fittings, that's all. The new engines we're working on are much lighter and far more reliable."

At the far end of the engine compartment was another door. Henrietta went through, only to find herself on a walkway that extended out into space. Beneath it, two enormous doors hinged out and were open downward.

"This is the forward hold. As you can see, it opens from the bottom. The assembly at the top has cables. We plan to winch cargo in directly because getting a crane inside would be difficult."

"Very clever, I must say," said Henrietta. At the far end was another door. "So what's next?"

"There is another engine compartment and the rear hold," said Uncle Robert. "They are just like the ones you've seen. Then at the stern, there is a third engine compartment, but it has only a single engine in it."

"So is that the tour?"

"Yes, unless you want to climb up through the rigging and get out on top."

"Could we?"

"No, not today. You aren't dressed for it." Her uncle was of course correct. A long skirt, even one for riding, would never do for climbing ladders.

Getting back down into the main cabin proved something of an adventure. Alexander had insisted on going first to be ready to catch Henrietta if she fell. Despite being careful, she of course caught her heel in her skirt and tumbled into his arms. He held her for a long moment, and she enjoyed the sensation. He was strong and powerfully built. With Alexander's arms about her and staring up into his face, she quite forgot herself for the moment. Then, realizing where she was, she blushed with embarrassment.

Uncle Robert peered down from above and saw the whole thing. Now, as if to add insult to injury, he said, "If you two can tear yourselves apart, I'd like to come down now."

Henrietta, not fully realizing what had happened, pulled back from Alexander with a start and mumbled, "I do so apologize."

For his part, Alexander smiled and said, "Think nothing of it, my lady. The pleasure of catching you in my arms was all mine." Then realizing what he'd said might be taken as overly forward, he dug the hole he was standing in deeper, saying, "I mean to say I'm glad I caught you and you didn't fall on your...err...and I'm an idiot." This just made Henrietta's color rise to an even brighter pink.

Uncle Robert started laughing out loud. "Alexander, I certainly hope you can fly an airship better than that." Then he took Henrietta's arm, placed it in his, and began walking the embarrassed girl to the door.

As they walked down the passageway between the staterooms, Henrietta impishly asked, "Uncle Robert, this is all so grand. Which of the staterooms will be mine?"

"Yours?"

"Yes, mine. You can't possibly expect that after seeing this wonder I am not going to go with you."

"Henrietta, dear..." her uncle began.

Henrietta turned back and grabbed Alexander's free arm. "I brought him back to you. I should have some reward...particularly if I can keep him occupied and prevent him from running off again." Her years of work with her mommy learning how to behave like a lady and still have her way paid off. No gentleman could have turned her down. But Uncle Robert was determined to try.

"Henrietta..."

Before he could say no, she quickly changed the subject, saying, "If you fly off and leave me all alone again, I just don't know how I could possibly survive. You simply must take me with you. Think of my reputation!"

She batted her eyes, and Uncle Robert gave up. "Fine. You may come along. Take whichever of the rooms suits you."

"Oh, thank you, Uncle Robert."

"On one proviso. You must promise to stay out of trouble and keep this young man from running off again."

Henrietta agreed. The three came down the gangway and walked out to Uncle Robert's shiny black automobile. "The office is a short distance from here, so we'll ride."

Henrietta eyed the automobile. "Uncle, may I ask another favor?"

"Now what?"

"I'd like to drive, if I may."

"Do you know how to drive?"

Henrietta lied. "Much to the distress of Mommy, meaning your sister, Beatrice, I had a friend teach me." In actuality she'd watched others drive and imagined that she could if given a chance.

"Well then, be my guest."

She got behind the wheel. She put her foot on the brake, checked all the gauges, noted the steam pressure, and moved the lever to the drive setting. As she let her foot off the brake cautiously, the automobile eased forward.

It turned out Henrietta was correct; she did know how to drive after all... that is, at least, drive across a flat open field in the middle of Oklahoma. Stopping was another matter. She stepped down far too hard on the brake pedal and nearly launched all three of them over the hood of the vehicle. Giggling, she said, "Not too bad for a first try."

"First try?" exclaimed Uncle Robert. "I thought you said you knew how to drive."

"No, I said someone had taught me how. I didn't say I knew how or had ever actually driven before."

Uncle Robert shook his head. "Well, at least we survived the attempt."

Alexander was laughing hard. "I, for one, am very impressed. I imagine next thing you know, you'll claim you know how to pilot an airship."

Henrietta didn't let the comment go without an answer and said, "No, not today. Perhaps tomorrow if I am not too busy."

Getting out of the vehicle, Uncle Robert said, "Henrietta, I'm going to need to borrow Alexander from you for a while. I need his help. I thought what you could do would be to spend some time with Mrs. VonKleist."

"Mrs. VonKleist? Who is that?"

"She's Alexander's wife. She's been helping out."

Henrietta looked at Alexander and said, "You're married? You are just full of surprises, aren't you?" It didn't come out the way she wanted it too. It sounded almost like she was jealous or disappointed. In reality, she was relieved. It wasn't that she didn't like him. Alexander was nice. It was just that until she found someone like the boy who wrote her treasured love letters, she just wouldn't be ready.

Before Alexander could answer, Uncle Robert said, "If you hadn't brought Alexander back, I don't know what we'd have done. Fergus MacGregor, our first officer, would have had to pilot the ship, and I can tell you…" Uncle Robert stopped before he said something he'd regret and finished with, "I'll just leave it at. I am so very pleased you brought Alexander back to us. I'm sure the others will be more than relieved to see him too."

Henrietta asked, "Where is Baroness VonKleist?"

"It's just Mrs. VonKleist."

"Then where is Mrs. VonKleist?"

"She's inside. I'll take you to her and introduce you. Then, after I get you settled, the boys and I can get back to work. We will all get back together at dinner this evening."

"But what am I to do in the meantime?"

"Oh, don't worry. I'm sure the two of you can find something."

Inside the office, Fergus and several men were seated and talking. On seeing Robert, they all stood. He began, "Gentlemen, I have good news. Our wayward pilot is back with us."

Fergus grinned and said, "Good job, mate. I see you even found a bonnie lass to bring back with you." Turning to Henrietta, he asked, "And who might you be, lassie?"

Alexander stiffened. "She is no mere lassie. She is the Lady Henrietta, daughter of the Earl of Hardingham, and Mr. Turnbull's niece. Show some respect."

Chastened, Fergus bowed his head and said, "I beg your pardon, Lady Henrietta. I meant no disrespect."

With just a hint of British propriety in her voice, Henrietta answered, "I should think not, particularly after I rescued and returned your captain and Commander to you." Then she giggled.

Fergus was about to begin another apology, but before he could speak, a woman burst in from the next room. She was no older than Henrietta. Her blonde hair left no doubt she was of Nordic-German ancestry. "I thought I heard a woman's voice," she said.

Alexander cleared his throat. "My lady, I have the honor of presenting my wife, Margaretha." Turning to Margaretha, he said, "Margaretha, I'd like to introduce you to Mr. Turnbull's niece, the Lady Henrietta Whitfield."

"It so nice to meet you," Margaretha said. "It will be nice to have a woman friend to talk to."

Alexander spoke up. "Dear, Lady Henrietta is a real English lady. She's not pretending."

"Oh dear, excuse me, my lady. I didn't mean to be so presumptuous…"

Henrietta cut her off. "Baroness VonKleist—I mean Mrs. VonKleist—don't be silly. You simply must consider me a friend. Please just call me Henrietta, as my friends do. After all, we are in America, and titles over here… they simply don't matter nearly as much as they do in Britain."

Uncle Robert grinned. "Well said, my dear. Now, with you two ladies settled, I need to borrow the men. We have work to do."

"No, Uncle, if I am to be part of this enterprise and not just a burden, I must help. Please tell me, what can I do?"

Margaretha smiled at her. "I like you. I've been saying all along that I should be allowed to help. I know just as much about the airship as any of them. Fergus and Alexander won't listen to me."

Uncle Robert was amused. "All right, young lady, if you think you can be of help, tell me, what can you do?"

Henrietta thought for a moment. "If you plan to go to London, you'll need a navigator. I just happen to be one."

Alexander asked, "You mean you can navigate just like you drive an automobile?"

"No, I mean I helped navigate our ship from Great Britain. I'll have you know, my calculations were even more precise than the captain's. He thought I was the best navigator he'd ever sailed with, particularly after I kept us from running aground off Nova Scotia."

Uncle Robert said, "Well, I'm not certain…"

"Ask my cousin James. He'll tell you the same thing."

The commotion had disturbed her cousin James. He came in, still wearing the bandage about his head. "Did I hear Henrietta?" he asked.

Henrietta jumped and ran to her cousin. "Oh, James, you are all right. I was so worried."

"I will be fine now that they've found you and you're safe. I'm sorry I didn't get back to you. The wind and the accident…"

"Don't worry about it. We are all here now, and all is well. Have you seen the airship?"

"Not yet, but Fergus and Margaretha told me all about it. It sounds wonderful."

"Oh, it is. The best part is that I am to be the navigator."

Uncle Robert then asked James, "Henrietta claims she is a navigator. Is that true?"

"Indeed. The captain of our ship from Britain took sick and left his first officer to navigate the ship. The man was a drunk and made a horrible mistake. Henrietta saw it, but the man was too much of a proud fool to admit it. He'd rather have run the ship aground than admit she was correct. Henrietta and I had to rouse the captain and show him the error. It kept us off Sable Island near Nova Scotia. It's a real dangerous place and is known as the graveyard of the Atlantic. After the captain took over, the first officer was locked in his cabin. Because the captain was so ill, Henrietta then navigated us the rest of the way to the harbor. She is really very good at it and saved the ship and everybody aboard."

Henrietta beamed. "See? I told you so!"

Uncle Robert smiled. "If you are that good, we'll need a good navigator. I think we'd be foolish not to make you part of the crew."

At this, Margaretha looked distressed and a little bit hurt. She whined, "I've been asking for days to go along and been told no! She shows up, and just like that, you say she gets to go and even be part of the crew and…the navigator no less! It's not fair!" Margaretha looked like she was about to start crying. "You can't leave me alone like this! I can help too! It is just so completely unfair!"

Henrietta had to agree; it wasn't fair. Thinking quickly, she said, "Of course you are coming. I am a single woman and cannot be expected to go flying off in the company of men without a proper chaperone. You will be my perfect companion."

At that, Margaretha lit up. "Oh, thank you, my lady. I can't tell you how much that means to me. Thank you so much."

"You are more than welcome. And as I said, we are friends, so please call me Henrietta."

Margaretha's husband, speaking as the captain, started to object. "Mr. Turnbull…Robert…do you really think a woman like my Margaretha is capable of being part of the crew, much less an officer?"

Robert dismissed the objection, saying, "Son, a woman is very capable of leading. Need I remind you that two of the greatest leaders of Great Britain were Elizabeth and Victoria?"

"But they were queens."

"It doesn't matter. We now live in the twentieth century. If you doubt the capacity of women, I suggest you look at Marie Curie, who is smarter than you are, and Annie Oakley, who is a better shot."

"But…"

"And Hetty Green, who has almost as much money as I did."

"I stand corrected."

"Yes, you do. More than that, you now have a new member of the crew to deal with. I am naming Margaretha a flying officer and assistant to our navigator." Turning to her, Robert added, "Congratulations, my dear."

Margaretha danced over and gave the older man a hug. "I promise you will not regret this kindness, sir—not ever!"

With the matter of Henrietta's and Margaretha's new roles settled, it was time for the team to sit down for their daily project meeting. It began with a report from Mr. Philip Andrew, the president of Uncle Robert's wholly owned airship subsidiary. "I am pleased to report that the final bills for fabrication of the structure came. It is slightly less than was budgeted."

Henrietta asked innocently, "Just how much would that be?"

Uncle Robert nodded, and Mr. Andrews told her. "For the whole ship, this site, and the one in England, roughly fourteen and a half million dollars, or about three million pounds."

Henrietta was shocked. "That's more money then there is in the whole world!"

Uncle Robert laughed. "No, my dear, it is not, but it is a sizable part of my fortune."

"Why have you spent so much? Can you ever possibly earn it back?"

"Oh yes, and many times more. This is more than just a single ship to prove a point. It is the first of a fleet of ships I have that we can operate ourselves or sell to the United States and Britain."

"A whole fleet. Oh my, I never ...please tell me about it."

"You may be aware the German Kaiser, Wilhelm II, appointed Rear Admiral Alfred von Tirpitz as his state secretary of the navy back in 1897. Together, they have been preparing for a great war to take control of Europe. What you may not know is that Germany plans to build a fleet of warships that will rival the Royal Navy. If their progress is as fast as some claim it is, the German fleet may have parity in ships in ten years, perhaps a lot fewer."

Henrietta was shocked. "Uncle, please tell me their plans aren't realistic."

"Sadly, they are. In addition to building regular warships, we have good reason to believe Count Ferdinand von Zeppelin is building a number of airships much like ours. It is because of these German efforts that we kept the project secret and have never announced its true purpose."

"What makes what the Germans are doing such a problem? Their airship can't be that dangerous."

"They can be and are because of bombs. They could use a ship like this to bomb London or even New York."

"Bomb from the sky?"

"Yes, but the trouble is that even from a stationary balloon, the wind carries a bomb a long way from any aiming point. If an airship is moving, there is no telling where the bomb might land."

"It doesn't sound like it would be every efficient."

"It wouldn't be, but if the Germans had enough airships and wanted to bomb an arms factory, for example, they could simply drop a whole lot of bombs everywhere around it, and some would surely hit it. In the process, they'd end up destroying everything around, meaning homes, schools, churches, everything."

"That's monstrous!"

"At first we thought so, particularly when we found out that right now, the Germans already have at least twenty ships and maybe a lot more."

"Dear me, that's frightening!"

"Henrietta, it is so much worse than even that."

"They have something worse? How could that be?"

Uncle Robert explained, "Working with Nikola Tesla's idea of a radio controller for an unmanned device and Reginald Fessenden's inventions for radio signal modulation, they've come up with a way to steer special aerial bombs to a particular target. Rather than a dumb bomb that goes, well, anywhere, it is a smart bomb that goes only where it is told. This means, for example, that they will have the ability to bomb British warships when we think they are safe in harbor. This will change the way wars of the future will be fought. It is simply a matter of whoso rules the sky rules the world. That is why I have been in secret negotiations with the president of the United States, my great and good friend, Theodore Roosevelt."

"You know the President?"

"I have known him since before his days as the Under Secretary of the Navy. We used to hunt together, but that is a story for another day. The president believes, as do I, in the benefits of leadership by the English-speaking world. He is fearful that the rise of the new German empire will eventually plunge the world into a war the likes of which has never been seen. For that reason, he and I have invited the British ambassador and representative of the Royal Navy to join with us. They, along with representatives of the US Navy, will witness a demonstration of this ship. They are all very interested in what this ship promises. More than that, they have placed orders for several ships. What we need to do is prove that it works. As I say, if it does, my investment will be returned to me many times over. It will also assure that Britain and the United States will be able to peacefully rule the sky and the waves, making a German war impossible."

"But how can a single airship make that much difference?"

"It is simple. The Germans must use explosive hydrogen gas to fill their ships. A single spark will set them on fire. We have helium gas, and our ships will not burn, no matter what. If we have a weapon like the ones they are building, that is to say smart bombs, it will be their airships and their navy that are at risk."

Chapter Four:
First Impressions

Uncle Robert realized the need to make a positive first impression to all those who they were meeting with in Washington. This was to be both the first airship of a great commercial line and the prototype for the great warships of the future.

Robert had never served in the Navy but had sailed on the great ocean liners. He recognized the value of having the entire crew, regardless of their particular job, skilled and familiar with every system that kept the ship in the air. To that end, he decreed that all who flew were to have training in every department, just as young officers in every great navy would have training in all shipboard matters.

He also recognized the value that uniforms and badges conferred. He had spent time planning how to present this ship and crew to the world. He wanted to make his crew's uniforms both familiar and distinctive at the same time. He rejected just copying the Navy uniform. It was too familiar and already being used by seagoing merchant ships. His airships were special. He decided the uniforms were to be black as he considered it more elegant than navy blue. Uncle Robert liked the look of the notched lapel on civilian suits and the patch pockets with button flaps of the Army officer's uniforms. He particularly liked the look of the recently adopted gorget patches on the lapels to indicate rank. One of the several fortunes Uncle Robert made was in silver mining, so all of the buttons and badges were silver. They included unique buttons, cap badges, and tie tacks.

Uncle Robert got a little carried away and went so far as to organize the new line as though it was a military service. The members of the fight crew were given ranks as commissioned officers. They included flight cadets (midshipmen or second lieutenant), flight officers (sublieutenant or first lieutenant), flight lieutenant (lieutenant or captain), flight leader (lieutenant commander or major), flight commander (commander or lieutenant colonel), captain (captain or colonel), commodore (commodore or brigadier). The commodore was to head the new line. For the moment, Robert claimed the title for himself: Commodore Turnbull. Thinking ahead, Uncle Robert also provided an armband to be worn on the left forearm of each commissioned officer's jacket naming the ship on which he served. Lastly, flying officers were to wear an eagle flying over the world above their left breast pocket—so-called flight wings. Ground crew wore the same uniforms but received no "wings."

It took three days to complete the final assembly of the ship and fill all of the gas bags. At dawn on the fourth day, all was ready. The airship *Cimarron* emerged into the morning light for the first time. The hull was silver-grey, but the vertical tails had been painted with a unique red, white, and blue design reminiscent of a flag fluttering. Prior to its launch, the ship's fuel tanks were filled, the galley provisioned, and all of Henrietta's navigation material loaded. The ship floated gracefully from the movable mooring mast.

Henrietta stood on the christening platform beneath the gondola. She was dressed in her new uniform. It befitted her status as the ship's second officer and navigator. Margaretha, a gifted seamstress, had remade two of Henrietta's riding habits into uniforms, one for herself and a second for Henrietta. Their long, black riding skirts matched and fitted ladies' jackets had the same unique buttons found on the men's uniforms. Margaretha's collar bore the tabs of a flying officer. Henrietta's had the more elaborate badges of a flight leader or lieutenant commander. A white high-collar blouse with black silk tie held in place with the special tie tack completed their looks.

The women required hats. They didn't want to look as if they were going fox hunting, so they rejected top hats. Margaretha and Henrietta tried standard black officer's peaked caps, but they thought the brim covered too much of their faces. Neither considered the look flattering. Lacking the service of a proper milliner, Margaretha took it upon herself to save the day. She started with a Glengarry cap worn by her father's old regiment, the Black Watch Highlanders. By combining the old military cap with a "pork pie hat" her grandmother wore, Margaretha fashioned a feminine but substantial cap out of black felt. She decorated the cap with the new airship line cap badge and a feather placed off center on the left side. It was both traditional and very modern. The ladies wore the hats with their hair pulled back into low chignons suitable for riding.

Uncle Robert was impressed with their ingenuity but was unwilling to adopt the new look for officers. He said, "I am delighted you young ladies have such a good eye for fashion, and if I were dressing girls to work as maids, I might agree. As it stands, if you are going to be flying officers, you'll wear a peaked cap like the other officers."

"Could we at least make the cap a little better looking than plain black?"

"How?"

"Maybe something shiny or, I don't know, just better."

"Give it a try. If the others will go along, I'll take a look."

They came up with a traditional cap highlighted with a silver-on-black band. The edge of the crown was piped with silver, and a modified eagle flew above the company badge centered above the brim. It was a tad gaudy for some but nonetheless acceptable and became standard headgear of the line.

On the christening platform, Henrietta stood with her Uncle Robert Turnbull, the ship's builder, the ship's commander, Captain Alexander Von-Kleist, and the first officer. An expensive bottle of champagne, saved for the occasion, was suspended from a ribbon tied to the ship above her. She, as the niece of the builder, was given the privilege of christening the ship. She swung the bottle and released it from her grasp. It flew forward and shattered. As it did, Henrietta said in a clear, loud voice, "I christen thee the *Lady Cimarron*!"

Uncle Robert sputtered, "You were supposed to just say 'the *Cimarron*.' What were you thinking?"

"But Uncle Robert, you've always talked about the ship as though it were a woman, and she is so beautiful....She just had to be a lady. Don't you agree?"

Alexander laughed. "Too late now, Robert. You can't change the name of the ship. It would be bad luck if you did."

"Harrumph. Then is...the *Lady Cimarron* ready to depart on her maiden voyage?"

When her uncle Robert declared that Henrietta was to be part of the crew, it had come as something of a surprise. When she was named navigator and second officer, it had nearly been too much. Flight Leader Cooke spoke for himself and the rest of the crew. He boldly stated, "We understood that, by rights, the navigator would be second officer and have the rank of flight leader, but..."

"But what?" Henrietta demanded.

"Ma'am...Lady Henrietta, you are a woman. You can't expect that we'll serve under your command."

Before her uncle could respond, Henrietta challenged them all. She pulled herself up and, with the distain of an offended British aristocrat, said, "And why not? Gentlemen, if any of you consider yourselves more fit than I to command, then prove it."

"How would we do that?"

"Well, as none of you know how to navigate, it will need to be something more manly. As we are in the Wild West, might I suggest riding, shooting, and cards?"

The men took up her challenge. It was a mistake. Henrietta was an experienced rider. She spoke to her horse in a whisper, then mounted and spurred it over the top rail of the corral's fence. Turning from riding to firearms, she set out six glass bottles on another section of fence. She said, "I believe the rules in a duel are ten paces, then turn and fire." She loudly counted off twenty steps, then turned and, with the little 32 caliber weapon she'd practiced with so fervently, broke them with six shots. None of her challengers had even the remotest hope of matching her performance.

Stepping back indoors and sensing victory, Henrietta suggested, "Shall we try our hands at cards?" She had spent her entire summer at age fifteen mastering card tricks. She cut the deck with one hand and then fanned the cards on the table. Hands flying, she demonstrated her skill. She turned over the ace of spades on the top of the deck, replaced it, then cut and shuffled the deck. She then showed them the ace again by turning over the top card. Replacing it, she cut and shuffled again, only to once more show the ace still on the top of the deck. As she performed, she innocently said, "I do so love playing cards, don't you? What shall we play? Perhaps poker?" Cutting and shuffling again, she revealed the ace for a fourth time and set the deck down. "Perhaps I could entice you to bet your britches you can beat me. But I think it only fair that I warn you: I cheat at cards." Fearing they were about to lose their remaining dignity, none of the men was willing to take up Henrietta's challenge, and with that, the objections ceased.

Over the next few days, each came to marvel at Henrietta and realize she was a force to be reckoned with. She was as smart and quick as any of them. She could outride and outshoot all of them, and no doubt cheat them at cards. On top of that, she was the daughter of an English earl and a proper lady. She was heiress to at least part of Robert Turnbull's incredible fortune so would be, if she wasn't already, fabulously wealthy. Everything in their world seemed as it should be, but the newspapers that Uncle Robert delivered told a different story. Europe was on the brink of war once again. Uncle Robert's fears might have been about to be realized.

On the day the *Lady Cimarron* was christened, she had taken flight for the first time. After the ceremony was over, Captain VonKleist climbed down the stairs from the platform. He turned back to offer his hand to Henrietta. She descended, followed by the first officer, then her uncle. They and the last of the crew boarded.

Once all were at their stations, Captain VonKleist seated himself. Then without fanfare, he gave the order: "Release moorings." The men below released their hold on the mooring lines, and the man at the bow let go of the attachment to the mooring mast. As the great vessel slowly began to rise, Alexander said, "Props dead slow astern." The ship slowly backed away from the mooring mast. Alexander next ordered, "Helm hard over port. Let the wind take her." The bow swung to the left. When the captain saw they were clear of the tower, he ordered, "Helm, steady as she goes. Props ahead slow. Flight, take us to six hundred feet relative." A chorus of acknowledgements followed. "Steady as he goes, aye."

"Ahead slow, aye."

"Six hundred feet relative, aye."

The faint sound of the propellers could be heard.

Alexander enjoyed the minute it took to reach altitude. Flight called, "Captain, six hundred feet steady."

Alexander answered Flight by name. "Thank you, Mr. Cooke." Turning over his shoulder, Alexander called on Henrietta. "Navigation, set course for St. Louis."

Henrietta spoke for the first time. "To St. Louis, aye. Bearing seven five true."

Helm answered her. "Navigation, zero seven five true, aye." Helm spun the wheel, and the ship turned to the heading.

Alexander waited until he heard, "Captain, steady on zero seven five true." Using Helm's name, Alexander said, "Thank you, Mr. Churchill."

Fight announced, "Captain, six hundred relative."

"Thank you, Flight." Then returning his attention to maneuvering the ship, Alexander addressed Props by name. "Mr. Reynolds, half ahead, if you please."

Props replied, "Half ahead, aye." In moments, the thrum of the ship's power could be heard and felt. After a few minutes, Alexander asked, "Navigation, what's our speed?"

Part of Henrietta's responsibilities as navigator was to monitor altitude, both absolute and relative to the ground. Another of her tasks was to monitor airspeed and ground speed. Only during mooring was speed important to Helm and Props. They all agreed that if only one or the other reading was requested, it should be specified. A general inquiry was to be responded to with airspeed first, followed by ground speed. An explanation of any difference was given at the navigator's discretion. Henrietta replied, "Speed forty and forty-seven, steady."

"Thank you, Miss Whitfield. Mr. Reynolds, ahead full. Let's see what the *Lady Cimarron* can do."

"Ahead full, aye." The thrum and rumble of the engines increased.

So it went for the next three hours. Alexander took the *Lady Cimarron* through its paces. Uncle Robert had started out on the bridge in an observer's seat but soon moved back into the main salon. He wanted to give every member of the crew a chance to be on the bridge for a time during the ship's maiden flight. Over the course of the flight, they traveled at the astonishing speed of seventy-four knots and as high as eight thousand three hundred feet above sea level. Over that part of Oklahoma, they were more than a mile above the high plains. They descended as low as a mere forty-six hundred feet above sea level or six hundred feet relative, or above the ground. That would be the typical operating altitude.

They changed course repeatedly. Flying in a great uneven circle, they at last returned to the field. A movable mooring mast rested on a double set of railroad tracks. In their absence, the ground crew pulled it a thousand yards out from the hangar. The ground speed dropped to nearly zero. Alexander, having given the order to moor, now sat in silence. The procedure demanded that the bridge crew coordinate their individual efforts. Each man had his own duties, and if crew members needed to speak, they did so directly to each other.

Henrietta continuously called out ground speed in feet per second. "Fifteen slowing…ten slowing…five slowing…"

Helm answered, "Stop ahead."

The man standing atop the mast grabbed a line dropped by a crewman from a hatch just below the prow and attached it to the steam-powered winch. The ship was drawn forward to an automatic coupler based on those used by the railroads. Once secure, the ship could swing gently in answer to the wind. Lines dropped from the gondola would hold the ship steady when the gangway was in use.

The triumphant crew cheered and waved to the ground crew, who were on the field to greet them. There was no time for a real celebration. So long as the ship remained out of its hangar, a watch crew would remain aboard to deal with any emergency. The *Lady Cimarron* was now their home. They had to take care of her. Over the next week, just as Uncle Robert ordered, all crew members took their turn at every station. By the time the week was out, all were equipped to do any task that might be required of them in the event of an emergency.

This included Henrietta and Margaretha. When the shakedown flights began, only Alexander had had any actual flight time. The two women could now boast as many hours in the air as any other member of the crew and, indeed, more hours in the air than any but a select group of fliers working for Count Zeppelin. Just like the other members of the crew, they were expected to know how to man every station. That included climbing into the rigging and out on top of the ship. Margaretha had reluctantly but gratefully embraced the clever convertible riding skirts Henrietta wore. They opened out and buttoned back. They were a delightful compromise to wearing men's trousers, something she, even as a married woman, was not prepared to do at that point. She was delighted with the freedom of movement the skirts allowed, and the fact that she didn't fall every time she used the ship's ladders was an added bonus. Even so, when not playing a "top man" in the rigging, she kept the full, long skirts buttoned to maintain the illusion of a regular dress. Henrietta told Margaretha, "How I had to struggle to convince Mommy that convertible skirts were not unladylike and fit only for circus people." That made Margaretha giggle.

Henrietta confided in Margaretha regarding her doubts about her own ability. "I don't know if I will ever learn all that is expected of me."

In reply, Margaretha scolded her, "Don't be ridiculous. You are so clever and already understand the difficult part. After all, you've studied mathematics and navigation. All I know about is what I've picked up from Alexander and his friends. It's mostly common sense stuff, not real learning."

With that in mind, Henrietta taught Margaretha the basics of navigation, and Margaretha taught Henrietta everything else. Their progress was rapid, so fast that by the morning of the third day, Alexander turned the ship over to Henrietta as officer of the watch, then silently observed her take the ship up on a two-hour flight and return to the mooring mast without incident.

The days were full of work and the evenings after dinner full of study. The hour in between was time to socialize. Henrietta loved hearing stories but even more loved to tell wild and fanciful tales. She would regale the men with stories she'd read. Such was her gift for imaginative gab, they nearly believed she had lived all of the adventures herself.

On the eighth day of flight operations, the first serious weather event began. Before day's end, it would come frighteningly close to killing them all. The day began with yet another practice flight. As they had flown east some sixty miles, the weather from the southwest began to darken. Flight Lieutenant Barnett, the radio operator, reported, "Captain, weather report from the field. They report they have a thundercloud wall coming from south-southwest."

"Very good, Mr. Barnett. Keep me posted."

A second report came in a few minutes later. "Captain, the field reports winds gusting to sixty and dollar-size hail."

"Very good, Mr. Barnett."

It was anything but very good. Everyone on the bridge knew a storm like this was dangerous. The wind and hail could tear them apart. A sudden change in pressure or wind direction could cost them lift and fling them to the ground. The storm might kill them by flinging them up so quickly, the gas bags could not be vented quickly enough, would overexpand, and then blow the ship apart. Even the immortality of youth might not protect them.

As they turned back to the field, the captain could see the storm ahead. It was a monster. His heart sank. He ordered the crew to weather stations. This was a drill they'd practiced but never used in earnest before. All crewmen had a station where they could observe a critical system or component. They stood by emergency manual vents and ballast release levers. Two engineers attended each engine. Men stood with block and tackle to control fins and rudders should control cables snap. Others were stationed with lights to spot damage to the hull. The first officer announced, "Captain, the ship is at weather stations."

"Very good, Mr. MacGregor."

In front of them was a solid wall of dark and threatening clouds obscuring the horizon. With no way to avoid it, Alexander turned the *Lady Cimarron* into the storm. "Helm, take her head into the wind. Props, half ahead. Flight…if you start to lose her, call it."

In a storm, Henrietta's post was the navigation station. Over a city or mountainous terrain, she would need to steer the ship clear of obstacles. Over the flat ground of Oklahoma, her primary task was to monitor and call out changes in relative altitude. For the minutes before they reached the clouds, it left her with little to do but worry.

Alexander and the other senior officers, including Henrietta, had held a meeting just two days earlier to discuss the type of situation they were now facing. "My standing orders," Alexander began, then paused and began again. "Our standing orders are, if a storm can be avoided, it will be avoided. If it cannot be avoided, we shall attempt to stay to the storm's edge. If we run into something too large to avoid, we will attempt to pass through it as quickly as possible. We must feel the winds like a bird. I have been up in a balloon during a storm. I can tell you that as we approach the leading edge, we will be facing strong updrafts and be pulled in. Do not be fooled. Once we pass into the storm and the heavy rain starts, the drafts will be down, and they will try to push us back and into the dirt. We must be ready to fight for lift, but the trick will be not to lose control of our ascent. If we do, we will rise too quickly and overpressurize the gas bags."

Flight Lieutenant Benjamin Reynolds, senior propulsion engineer, or Props, asked, "Do we accelerate as we enter?"

"No, I think that we keep our steam pressure up but hold at half ahead until we need it. Then we go to full emergency power."

"What about pressure in the bags?" asked Flight Leader Sebastian Cooke, senior flight dynamics engineer, or Flight.

"We'll need lift, but give yourself as much room with the bags as you can. Henrietta, as navigator, you'll watch our relative altitude and keep Sebastian from grounding us. Give us only our relative altitude unless you are asked for more." Flight Lieutenant John Churchill, chief helmsman, or Helm, looked concerned. Alexander smiled. "John, just keep her head in the wind the best you can. You'll have to feel your way."

They'd all practiced their jobs in clear air and fair skies. Now they were about to be put to the test. Henrietta recalled the many talks she'd had with her friend, the retired sea captain who had taught her navigation. He'd regaled her with stories about storm seas. He always told her, "If the storm is bad enough, even brave men will panic. It is the officers' job to remain calm no matter what is happening. There is always a better option than to run in circles and scream, 'We're all going to die,' so you must keep your head." She knew that whatever else might happen, she would never let herself scream or start to cry.

The beast they now faced was not one that could be avoided or would allow one to pass by untouched. They could see the flashes of lightning in the black, boiling clouds. As they approached, the wind picked up and pulled the *Lady Cimarron*. She started to rise. As they passed into the storm, the sky became black, and the ship started to buck and shake. They could hear the groan of metal.

Henrietta was the picture of composure on the outside. Inside, her stomach did somersaults, and her heart threatened to burst. The wind changed as heavy rain began pelting the ship. Now the storm threatened to fling them to the ground. Calmly, Henrietta intoned, "Altitude relative, nine hundred, down....Relative, eight hundred, down....Seven hundred, down." Henrietta's voice was soothing and steady and betrayed no hint of stress. Inside, she was terrified, but her training as an English aristocrat demanded she keep "a stiff upper lip."

Alexander ordered, "Flight, up bubble ten degrees. Props, full ahead, emergency."

"Flight up ten, aye."

"Ahead full, emergency, aye."

The engines surged to their maximum power. "Six hundred, down," said Henrietta. The nose of the *Lady* rose, but she was sinking to the ground. "Five hundred, down....Four hundred, down....Three hundred, down." Still there was no suggestion of concern in Henrietta's voice. "Two hundred, down." Alexander held his breath. Henrietta swallowed hard. "One hundred, down."

Flight called out with a hint of panic in his voice, "We'll hit by the stern."

Alexander blanched and braced himself. "Sound collision!" The collision horn bleated its warning.

Henrietta stared at her gauges and held her breath. She counted the seconds in her head: *One, two, three...* After what seemed to be an eternity, she at last exhaled. Calmly she said, "Fifty...steady."

Alexander took a breath of his own as did everyone on bridge. A moment later, Henrietta said, as though nothing had happened, "Two hundred, up."

The ship began to climb. It went all the way to two thousand five hundred feet relative before Flight regained control of the ascent. They ran through some light hail, and then the storm began to slacken. In an hour, the storm was astern. They had flown through the gates of hell and survived.

Days earlier, the *Lady Cimarron* had been spotted in flight, and the newspapers were going mad to get the story. Uncle Robert had finally given in, deciding it was time to reveal the ship to the world. At the suggestion of the president, the three major wire services were contacted and each asked to send a daring reporter willing to participate in a great adventure. The men were brought to the Cimarron Strip by train. Uncle Robert reopened his house, and they remained there overnight.

The next morning, the *Lady Cimarron* left early. By the time the men were up and fed, the ship was out of sight. Uncle Robert had them driven over in his steamer. At the site, they were struck by the size of the hangar. Uncle Robert took them into the field office. There, he told them of the scope of the Project. The reporters were understandably skeptical. "Do you really expect us to believe that such a ship could exist? If it does, where is it?"

As Uncle Robert was about to field their questions, a member of the ground crew stuck his head in. "Mr. Turnbull, excuse me for interrupting. You said you wanted to know when the *Lady* was coming in."

"Thank you. Gentlemen, if you will follow me, I will show you the ship."

The *Lady Cimarron* was nearly overhead. The reporters' mouths dropped open with amazement.

"Gentlemen, the *Lady Cimarron* will be moored in the next few minutes. After that, I'll be glad to introduce you to her crew. Perhaps after that, those of you who wish to may go aboard and take a tour. I'm sure Captain VonKleist and the crew would be glad to show you around."

The ship safely moored and the senior officers descended the gangway. Everyone knew that the press was expected and that tonight was to be a celebration and farewell. As they walked from the gangway, Flight Leader Cooke asked Henrietta, "Ma'am, may I have a word?"

"Certainly, Sebastian." They turned and walked a short distance away from the others.

"Ma'am, Lady Henrietta, I owe you an apology."

Looking into his beautiful brown eyes, she said, "Sebastian, whatever do you mean? And you needn't call me Lady."

"Yes, ma'am, I do. I doubted you were up to being crewman, and I said… well, I apologize."

"Don't worry about it. That was a long time ago."

"Ma'am, it's more than that. Today during the storm, I have to tell you, I was…well, I was scared. But you…you were magnificent. You remained so calm, so brave, you gave me—heck, all of us—the courage to get through it. Ma'am, you are the finest officer I've ever…well, I'd be honored to serve with you on any ship."

"Sebastian, dear Sebastian, I do believe that is nicest thing anyone has ever said to me." With a big smile, she took his arm. "Now, we'd better join the others."

As they walked, Henrietta whispered, "You're right. It was scary, but it is easy to be brave when you have someone like you looking out for us." Sebastian looked a little embarrassed. Henrietta saw his distress. She laughed and said loudly, "Oh, Mr. Cooke, you are so kind and such a gentleman."

As they moved across a bit of uneven ground, Henrietta nearly stumbled. Instinctively, she pulled closer to him and then continued to walk very close by his side as they went into dinner. Sebastian wasn't the only one aboard who was impressed by Henrietta's coolness in a crisis. Everyone, in fact, was impressed with "their lady."

Sebastian Cooke was a very bright and handsome young man. He came from a seafaring family. His father served the Royal Navy and had recently attained the rank of rear admiral. He was Navy to the core as had been his father, grandfather, and great-grandfather before him. Sebastian was a true disappointment to his father. He had refused to join the Navy, having far more interest in science and engineering than the quarterdeck. His broken-hearted father sent him off to boarding school and focused on his younger brother, who was interested in a naval career. Eventually Sebastian found his way to university. From there he moved on to work for Robert Turnbull. His work with gasses and the rudimentary principles of lighter-than-air flight landed him a position with the Cimarron Project. He was easily qualified to serve as props, helm, or even captain. The reason he did not want any of those jobs was simple—flight dynamics was the art of keeping a ship airborne, and it fascinated him. After Sebastian turned it down, Uncle Robert offered the job of captain to Alexander because he'd actually flown before.

Sebastian was without question the most skilled and the best-educated of all the other officers. Uncle Robert next urged Sebastian to consider becoming first officer. Sebastian declined the offer when he realized that it meant he would be required to divide his time between command duties, including standing watch, and working on flight systems. He argued he needed to be free to move about and work where he was needed. He also declined the role of second officer for the same reason, arguing it should be the job of the navigator. He accepted the rank of flight leader only as a compromise. Uncle Robert threatened to leave him on the ground unless he agreed to accept a commission and supervise the flight station on the bridge. Having been given no alternative if he wanted to fly, Sebastian gave in. Up until recently, the practical details of lighter-than-air flight fascinated him more than anything else. Now that he'd met Henrietta, flight had become far less important because he was completely and hopelessly smitten with her.

The senior officers and Margaretha entered the dining room. It was packed and brightly lit. As many of the ground crew as would fit had packed in. Uncle Robert made the introduction. "Gentlemen, may I present the senior officers of the *Lady Cimarron*. This is Captain VonKleist; First Officer MacGregor; Second Officer, the Lady Henrietta; and Flight Leader Cooke."

The reporters were taken aback. One asked without directing it at anyone in particular, "A woman as second officer?"

Captain VonKleist answered, "Yes, certainly. Lady Henrietta is our navigator."

Another reporter asked, "Lady Henrietta?"

Henrietta answered, "I am the daughter of the late 6th Earl of Hardingham and cousin to the present 7th Earl."

Robert quickly added, "She is also my niece and heir to my fortune, but it is her skill and not her family connections that have earned her the rank and position."

Alexander was captain, but he and the others might as well have been chopped liver. The reporters knew a good story when they heard one. After they learned of Henrietta's performance during the storm, they instantly denominated her the "Queen of the Sky." It was she who conducted the tour of the ship and told of its wonders. She even extended an offer that they come aboard and fly to Washington. By the end of the evening, the stories were already being written in the reporters' minds. They told of the marvelous airship, the *Lady Cimarron*, and the brave lady who flew her. It was because of these stories and those that followed that rigid airships quickly became known as *Cimarrons*.

After the reporters were escorted off to collect their luggage, Henrietta collapsed in her cabin. There was a tap at the door. "Come in."

It was Margaretha. "I know you're tired, but if we are really going to Washington in the morning, I need your help pinning the dress you gave me; otherwise, it won't fit properly."

"Oh, we can use the rear observation cabin if you can get your husband to chase all the men off."

"He's already doing it. Since you put up such a fit the other day about how much you dislike smoking, no one goes in there out of respect for you."

The ladies adjourned to the observation cabin. Henrietta wasn't dainty but was very fit and thin. Margaretha was hardly a big woman but still had to let the dress out. If she hadn't, she'd have been able to get into it but would not have been able to breathe. As Henrietta helped pin the dress back together, Margaretha said, "You and Mr. Cooke make a very handsome couple."

"A couple? We're not a couple."

"That's not what it looked like."

"Looked like when?"

"When you walked in holding onto him like you'd never let go of him."

"It was slick and wet outside. I didn't want to fall. That's all."

"That's what you say now, but—"

"But nothing! Oh, stop it."

At that, Margaretha giggled. "Just imagine—Mrs. Henrietta Cooke."

"Margaretha, if you don't stop it this instant, I'll have you put off the ship, and we'll go to Washington without you!"

When the dress was pinned, Henrietta went back to her cabin. *Now I've done it!* she thought to herself. She liked Sebastian Cooke. He was just the sort of a guy any girl would be interested in, but then so was Alexander. *Oh dear, now what am I going to do?* As she pondered, there was another knock on the door. "Come in."

The door opened, and it was Uncle Robert. "May I come in?"

"Certainly, Uncle, please do."

Uncle Robert indicated that she should sit. He sat across from her. "Henrietta, you are the daughter I never had, so you will have to forgive me if I don't know how to say this."

"Say what?"

"Well, it's about Mr. Cooke."

"I don't understand."

"I've seen the way he looks at you. One of the reasons it is not a good idea to have a woman on a ship is that the men, the young men, tend to fight over women."

"But Margaretha—"

"Margaretha is married. You are not. You well know most all of the young men are interested in you."

"Oh dear!"

"I know. That is why I am going to ask you for a favor. Please tell them the truth. They are your friends and your crewmates. You owe it to them."

"But Uncle…"

"If you are interested in one of them, tell him, or tell him you're not. Be honest with him. This is too important to play silly boy–girl games. It's far too easy to give someone the wrong idea. You can't play one of them against another. I…we need all of them."

"But Uncle Robert, I'd never…"

"I know that, my dear. But you must be careful."

"I will. I promise."

Henrietta had a difficult time falling asleep. Sebastian and the others were interested in her. Alexander stood a foot taller than Henrietta. He was very strong and powerfully built. He appeared the very embodiment of a Teutonic godlike being. Blonde, blue-eyed, and dashingly handsome, he was a born leader, strong and brave. Margaretha was lucky she'd nabbed him. Sebastian was handsome but not as large and powerfully built as Alexander. Nevertheless, he was hardly a weakling. Sebastian's more studious countenance distinguished him. Both men were athletic, but their choice of sports said worlds about them. Alexander preferred the rough and tumble of American football while Sebastian favored the serenity of English cricket. As nice as they were, thanks to the love letters and her active imagination, she knew neither of them was the man of her dreams.

The morning brought clear skies, and shortly after seven, they began breakfast. Before sitting down, Alexander asked Henrietta to talk privately. His message was very clear. "I know that last night, Mr. Turnbull spoke to you just as he did to me. He is a very wise man and has spotted a problem before it has begun. Henrietta, Sebastian and the others are your crewmates—"

Henrietta interrupted. "Alexander, you don't have to—"

"Yes, I do. So long as we are on the ship, we have a job to do. It must come first. There will be opportunities on the ground to pursue other matters, but those things cannot interfere with us in the air. Henrietta, if you like someone, you must put it aside when we are in the air. We must always remain crewmates first."

Henrietta nodded in agreement. She then took Alexander's arm as he escorted her in to breakfast.

An hour later, they were away. The first stop was to be at the World's Fair in St. Louis. The press had been able to send telegraph messages ahead, and Uncle Robert had thought to have a mooring mast erected just north and west of the fairgrounds. The *Lady Cimarron* appeared in the afternoon sky and slowly flew about to give all on the ground a good look before coming in to moor for the night. Thousands turned out to greet her, and a lucky few hundred actually got a tour. Once again, the press focused on the second officer, marveling that such a pretty young woman could be involved with such an adventure. Pictures of the Lady Henrietta were printed alongside pictures of the *Lady Cimarron*. A casual observer, upon seeing the illustrations, might have been forgiven if he or she believed the lady had invented the ship and flew it on her own.

Initially, Henrietta was happy to talk to the press. She spoke of the *Lady Cimarron* and her crew. She told of her late father and mommy. She spoke of her life growing up in both America and Great Britain. Reporters, being reporters, wanted more. One asked, "Lady Henrietta, what do you feel about the women's suffrage movement?"

Henrietta joked in reply, "Sir, I am not a political person, but I do consider women every bit as capable as men except in matters of childbirth, at which we excel and at which men are at a disadvantage." The comment brought the hoped-for chuckle to everyone present. At that, Henrietta raised her hand and said, "Gentlemen, I think that's enough for one day," ending the interview.

Some of the reporters wanted to continue, but Sebastian, who was with her, said, "Please, gentlemen, the young lady has had enough torment for today. If you have any further questions, you may address them to Mr. Turnbull or to me."

Henrietta took the opportunity to leave the room. Having escaped the clutches of the press once, she resolved she would not subject herself to them again unless ordered to.

Chapter Five:
Across the Sea

The situation in Europe was desperate. Fighting seemed inevitable. A trade war between Serbia and the Austro-Hungarian Empire had broken out. The strain between the two grew very much worse when the empire made an epic miscalculation. Serbia's great benefactor and ally, Russia, was embroiled in a nasty war with the Japanese. It seemed they would be unlikely to concern themselves with whatever went on in the Balkans. Emperor Franz Joseph considered Croatia part of his empire. It had been nominally a separate state but had been under the Austro-Hungarians' control since 1813. The Croatian city of Pula, with its natural harbor, became the main naval base of the Austro-Hungarian navy in 1859. Emperor Franz Joseph considered that with the Russians distracted, now was an opportune moment to formally annex Croatia. That action infuriated the Serbians, who had had eyes on Croatia themselves.

An appeal to the Russian tsar fell on deaf ears. The tsar had lost his only son, Alexei Nikolaevich, who had been born with hemophilia and died within days. The tsar refused to become involved. Without hope of Russian intercession, the most radical of the Serbians set upon the business of exacting revenge on their own. That took the form of sinking the Austro-Hungarian battleship in the harbor at Pula. Using a unique manned torpedo, two men snuck in and sank the SMS *Habsburg*. Unfortunately, the saboteurs were caught before they could escape. They claimed they had acted on their own. However, under questioning, they revealed they were officers in the Serbian army.

Taking his cue from the Americans' response to the sinking of the battleship *Maine*, the emperor declared war. By his reckoning, the Russians were so bogged down in their dispute with Japan, they would not dare come to Croatia's aid. Russia, though duty-bound by treaty to do so, surprised everyone, not the least Franz Joseph, by declaring war on Austria-Hungary. Germany was drawn in by reason of its alliance with the Austrians. That triggered France's treaty obligation to Russia, and they too were drawn in. The shooting had not yet begun, and there was still hope that bloodshed could be avoided.

Uncle Robert soldiered on. When asked what he thought about the international situation, he said, "Gentlemen, please, I am happy to talk about business and science as I have some experience in those matters, but that certainly doesn't make me an expert on everything. I will speak only of those things I know about and let others speak to matters they are more knowledgeable about than I." He refused to make any comment on the goings on in Europe.

When the reporters finally left, Robert came into the main salon where Henrietta and Margaretha sat together talking. His niece asked him, "Uncle, I know you didn't say anything to the reporters, but what do you think about what is going on in Europe? Will there really be a war, and will Britain and America be drawn into it?"

Uncle Robert pursed his lips, thinking. Then he said, "I do not know the particulars of what the Germans may be doing, but I will say the *Lady Cimarron* represents a great new advance in science. Ships like her carry the promise of a future filled with safe and reliable air travel all over the world. But there is a dark side, and ships like ours can become weapons, fearsome weapons. Just know that whatever the future may hold, I have already offered the gas we discovered and my expertise to both the British and American governments. To that end, I intend to fly the *Lady Cimarron* to Washington, where I will be meeting with the president and the British ambassador. After that, we'll head for London."

As her uncle spoke, Henrietta found herself growing cold. When Uncle Robert excused himself so he could get some rest, she and Margaretha remained. "A war," she whispered. "It sounds like a bad dream."

"It does, but don't worry. We're all in this together, and we'll get through whatever may be coming."

They sat in silence for several minutes, lost in thought. Henrietta then stirred. "Margaretha, tomorrow will be a very long day. I think we should go to our cabins and get some rest."

Margaretha nodded but remained in the salon for another hour before going to her husband and their own bunk.

At first light, Captain VonKleist gave the order, "Up ship," and they were away. A little over eleven hours later, they arrived over the Capitol building. Again, Uncle Robert had planned ahead, and a mooring mast across the Potomac awaited them. Uncle Robert and the senior crew arrived at the White House at eight thirty. It was a lavish affair. On the flight across the country, Uncle Robert warned Henrietta, "TR is an avowed reformer and progressive, but sometimes he has difficulty reconciling his Victorian worldview with the demands of you girls who are women of the twentieth century. He'll be impressed when I introduce you as both navigator and second officer, but don't be too distressed over how he reacts."

"What do you think he will?"

"We have a mutual friend, a junior diplomat named Cecil Spring-Rice. He's a great admirer of TR and was his best man at his wedding to the First Lady. Anyway, he'll be the first one to tell you that at his core, the president is about six years old."

Henrietta giggled. "A six-year-old! Do you actually expect me to talk to him as though he is a child?"

"Talk about riding, shooting, and your love of the outdoors. Tell him that life is a grand adventure if you let it be, and he'll do the rest."

True to her uncle's words, the president very quickly came to admire the spunky young English-American. She considered it the highlight of the evening when he said to her, "Bully for you, Henrietta. You are indeed the best of both worlds. If women truly want to be viewed as equals, they should follow your example! Bully for you!"

When one of the guests brought up Henrietta's unladylike skill as a card player, President Roosevelt opined that as a mere woman, she wouldn't present a real threat at the table even if she cheated.

She reprimanded him by saying, "Well then, sir, if you consider yourself so skilled that I will not be able to beat you, perhaps we should play cards? Although I suggest you simply give me your money now and avoid the embarrassment of having me take it from you later."

The tiger-bright gleam in her eye put the president off. Thinking the better of his comment, he apologized. Later, Henrietta whispered in confidence to him, "I know it was wicked to say such a thing. The truth is, I don't know how to play poker at all."

The laughter that followed was a mystery to everyone as was TR's booming comment, "No, my dear young lady, you know more about poker than I would ever try to match!"

As the evening progressed, Henrietta was pigeon-holed first by one person then another. Uncle Robert was busy dealing with the president and the politicians. Captain VonKleist was mobbed by the admirals. One by one, the men would break away from the group and crowd around her. At last, it was Rear Admiral Sir John Cooke who took a turn.

Sir John was beaming as he walked over to where Henrietta stood with his son. "Sebastian, my boy, that uniform suits you well." Then turning to Henrietta, he said, "But not nearly so well as yours suits you, Lady Henrietta."

"Thank you, Admiral Cooke. You are too kind."

"Not at all. As I understand it, you have earned that rank of flight leader." He then smiled at his son. "And for someone who said he'd never be interested in wearing a uniform…"

"Father…please."

"I am pleased. That is all. Very pleased. But I must say I like seeing you in that uniform."

Sebastian smiled in acknowledgement and then told his father, "Mr. Turnbull and the president have cooked up a treat for you when you take a ride on our ship tomorrow."

"What might that be?"

"Oh, it is their surprise, so I can't say." He the added quietly, "Father, as you watch tomorrow, I'd appreciate it if you'd remember that what we are doing is not a threat to the Navy. Far from it. If it all works out, it will be just something else making it stronger and better, like adding armor and steam."

"I'll keep that in mind."

The party continued until midnight. The demands upon Uncle Robert and Alexander kept them very busy. It had fallen to Sebastian to remain at Henrietta's side and provide what assistance she might need. Her training by Mommy made assistance unnecessary. Having dealt with the lecherous members of the British aristocracy, the efforts of a bunch of well-meaning "colonials" presented very little challenge. Still, she appreciated Sebastian's attentions. At one point, just after she ran off a congressman, she whispered to him, "Sebastian, I do so appreciate having at least one true gentleman whom I can count on with me in these travails."

That brought a grin to his otherwise somber and protective countenance. "Always, Henrietta. You may count on me always."

The evening finally over, they went back to the ship. As had become their practice, Margaretha and Henrietta sat together for a time in the main salon. They liked to collect themselves and talk over the day's events while sipping a cup of mild green tea. Henrietta drank coffee in the morning with Alexander, but at night she needed to rest, and coffee after dinner kept her up.

There was a big day planned. At just after nine, the motor car carrying the president arrived at the field. Behind him came the cars with the secretary of the Navy, the British ambassador, and a number of admirals. If there had been any fear of flying, none was expressed. If a young lady could do it, how dangerous could it be?

After a brief tour, the captain gave the order to up ship, and by noon they had traveled down the Chesapeake Bay and out over the Atlantic. Uncle Robert had done the Germans and their smart bombs one better. The weapon was not just smart, but it could be used against moving targets. The US Navy had been secretly ordered to provide towed targets for a demonstration. Most of the guests had no idea what they were about to see. Below, the targets were being pulled by destroyers at better than twenty-five knots. The two dozen guests aboard were seated in the main salon.

Robert explained, "Gentlemen, in a few minutes we will be in position to begin a demonstration attack. As you know, we believe the Germans are building special bombs that can be guided. We too have such a weapon. The Navy has been kind enough to provide two towed targets. Each is towed behind a destroyer and travelling at twenty-five knots or more. You will witness with your own eyes how effective this ship and its new weapons are. If all works as planned, you will see that our weapons are guided and can be used against moving targets. I will remind you that the warheads on these practice bombs are real. If one gets off course, we will detonate it in the air to avoid damaging the ships."

A young member of the crew stuck his head in. "Captain says we've sighted the targets ahead to port. We will begin our attack as soon as we've closed the distance."

"How long?"

"Captain said about eight minutes from now."

Out of the port window, the guests could see the wakes of the destroyers pulling the targets. A slight haze obscured the *Lady Cimarron* from view, but within a minute, the crews of the destroyers spotted her. The ships were at maximum speed but attempted to angle away from each other without losing headway. Relentlessly, the much faster *Lady Cimarron* ran them down. The bomb aimers sat in the small cabin just behind the bridge. From there they employed aiming devices that allowed them to visually track weapons in the air and steer them to target.

Alexander asked, "Navigation, what is our altitude?"

Henrietta answered, "Altitude six thousand relative and true."

From Flying Officer Johnson the call came, "Tracking two targets bearing relative three two zero, ten thousand yards. We have solutions."

"Very good, Mr. Johnson. Engage at your discretion."

"Engage at discretion, aye." The bomb aimers did the rest. A moment later, Mr. Johnson said, "Fox one away."

The *Lady Cimarron* shuddered slightly as it released its burden. The term *fox* was an abbreviation for *flying ordinance experimental. One* indicated it was the first weapon dropped. "Fox two away" was heard as the ship shuddered again.

Alexander ordered, "Helm, starboard sixty degrees. Let's give our passengers a good look. Props, half ahead."

"Sixty degrees starboard, aye"

"Half ahead, aye."

Henrietta added, "New course two, two, zero true."

"Navigation, two, two, zero true, aye."

From the port side windows, the president, the secretary of the Navy, the British ambassador, and the several admirals could all see the tail flairs of the weapons burning bright. Inexorably they fell. In moments, the first of the towed targets disappeared in a plume of water and smoke. Five seconds later, the second target silently disappeared. Only then did the sound of the first explosion reach them. The men were stunned. Admiral Schofield, the chief of naval operations, stood shaking his head.

Uncle Robert reassured him and the others, saying, "I am not a naval person, but I have read history and know that in war, foreknowledge of your opponent's action is always an advantage. What you have just seen does not mean the end of the surface fleet or the Navy...no, not any more than the advent of steam and the torpedo boats. No airship can replace big, powerful ships. They can, however, serve as part of the larger fleet, protecting large ships as destroyers do. They also have the added advantage of altitude. Imagine being able to see over the horizon when your enemy cannot, attacking them at a distance and closing upon them for decisive battle only when you chose, never again to be drawn into a battle of encounter. Think also, should an enemy try to hide from you by moving inland, that you will now have a means to follow them and run them to ground. Admirals, far from marking the end of the Navy, these ships—and make no mistake these are ships—will assist the Navy in becoming the dominant branch in any future conflict."

Uncle Robert could not have made a group of sailors any happier, Admiral Cooke most of all. His son had just given his old man even more of a reason to be proud. During the flight back to Washington, it was made clear that the president was going to seek funds from Congress to buy a fleet of ships. Uncle Robert agreed to the proviso that a similar opportunity be given to Great Britain, pointing out, "The British are likely facing a war with Germany. If they are able to buy my ships and, more importantly, the gas to fill them, and in exchange agree to allow the American fleet to make use of their bases around the world, we together can make the rest of the world behave itself."

That evening, there was a reception at the British embassy. Everyone who was anyone in Washington was there. The one notable exception was the German ambassador. He had not been invited to even so much as tour the *Lady Cimarron*. This omission had been deliberate and at the suggestion of the president and British ambassador.

The ambassador knew of the kaiser's and Count Zeppelin's fleet and had hoped to see what the opposition was up to. The report that the ship was fast and fireproof seemed a fantasy. He laughed when he saw her, noting, "She can't be built for speed. She hardly has the hull of a racer. Look at her lines! The hull looks short and fat. It looks more like what the Americans call a football than a warship. It's nothing more than a misshapen balloon. Where are the smooth, long, straight sides of Count Zeppelin's ships?" He also laughed at the claim she was fireproof. He first believed the story had been cooked up by the British to forestall any action against the ship. He became convinced when he learned that Uncle Robert had banned smoking aboard, claiming it bothered his niece. "Real men don't behave like that." He telegrammed his government, telling them of his findings.

The reception at the British embassy was a grand affair, and once again Uncle Robert and Alexander were pulled aside repeatedly to discuss options and plans. This left Sebastian to protect Henrietta from the unwanted advances of several men. The crew finally made it back to the ship, and Henrietta was truly grateful beyond measure. She complained, "I've had to smile so much over the last couple of days. Much more of it and...I'll never be able to smile again!"

Sebastian saw she was tired, so he tried to comfort her at first by saying, "But it is such a lovely smile."

Henrietta frowned and glared at him in disapproval. Sebastian was still sympathetic, but with her making a face like that, he couldn't resist the temptation to tease her. Looking as pathetic as he could manage, he added, "Well, at least the sun and moon will be glad to hear that they will no longer need to compete with the Queen of the Sky to light the world." That made Henrietta giggle, even though she didn't want to. Tired as she was, it took a second cup of green tea with Margaretha to settle her enough to fall asleep.

The next day was spent secretly preparing for the trip to London. Local weather conditions made departure at six in the evening desirable. Captain VonKleist ordered up ship at six thirty. The *Lady Cimarron*'s destination wasn't announced, but unconfirmed rumors reported in the newspapers indicated it was to be Canada. By eight, they were alone in the darkness over the North Atlantic.

While they flew, the world exploded. The Germans marched into Belgium the next morning. Great Britain stayed out of the war until the Germans refused to withdraw from little Belgium. Instead, they used Zeppelin's airships to deliver specially designed penetrator bombs developed to destroy the heaviest concrete fortifications. They had almost been a mistake. During prewar tests, the Germans had concluded their large eight-inch cannons were not capable of inflicting a fatal blow to the Belgian and French bunkers protecting their forces. In frustration, the general in charge of the test had reprimanded the engineers from Krupp: "If the shells won't do the job, you might as well throw the cannons at them." The engineers had done just that. Starting with an eight-inch cannon barrel, they built a smart bomb known as a *harpoon*.

The German weapon easily penetrated more than fifteen feet of unreinforced concrete. The forts at Liege were protected by ten to twelve feet of concrete at most. All twelve forts were destroyed in a single hour, and by the end of the third day of fighting, the Germans were across the Meuse and racing toward Namur.

As the *Lady Cimarron* sighted land, word of the German air attacks and lightning-fast advances were on everyone's lips. Uncle Robert had feared the worse. Anticipating the arrival of an unknown ship might be viewed with alarm. He'd included several large Union Jacks aboard. These were flown two at a time from poles extended from the gondola. Clearly visible from the ground and accented by the red, white, and blue tail colors, they helped frightened onlookers realize the ship was "one of ours." The faint sound of cheers could be heard even above the engines whenever passing over the throngs of well-wishers gathered to greet them.

Chapter Six:
Transatlantic Triumph

The *Lady Cimarron* traveled to a mooring mast and hangar located on Uncle Robert's large estate. A second hangar was nearing completion. The mast and hangars were located in Northumberland, generally in the vicinity of where Robert's ancestors had made their home. He'd acquired the house, known as Ruxmour Manor, just a few years earlier. The building was incomplete when he'd purchased it. Uncle Robert saw its potential, redesigned it, and made it into something unique. Work was still proceeding but had progressed to the point that his sister, the Dowager Countess Hardingham, could make it her home. The main house was a Gothic revival stone castle featuring embattled parapets and three-story towers at the corners. Outwardly, it resembled Syon House in London.

The interior of the house was impressive. The entrance hall, with its fine marble floor and uncluttered walls, opened directly into the main hall, which in turn opened into a great two-story-high, glass-enclosed atrium that doubled as the ballroom. It dominated the center of the house. The atrium was originally intended to be an open winter garden courtyard. Uncle Robert added a raised marble floor, installed the glass ceiling, and finished the space with a massive chandelier. On the far side of the atrium, a passage through a dual curved staircase gave access to the long gallery across the rear of the house. From there, guests could look out to the landing field in the distance.

Uncle Robert did not like overly ornamented furnishings. He believed form should follow function. The house was filled with simple but elegant furnishings, including deeply cushioned chairs and couches. Several stained glass windows and numerous Tiffany lights added a degree of color and warmth to the interior of what otherwise would have been a cold stone building. Together, it all made the building a comfortable and very livable home and not merely a showpiece to impress others.

The four principal suites and six large guest bedrooms were located on the second floor. Each had a private bath. Servants' quarters were also located in the partially complete section. The house was a lot to manage by a staff of only eight. Until the servants' quarters were completely finished, there was no room for more staff without severe overcrowding.

As the *Lady Cimarron* moored, she was greeted by a swarm of excited civilians and a few reporters. On any other day, this event, the first crossing of the Atlantic, would have brought banner headlines, but with the war on everyone's mind, the story in the *Times* was relegated to page fourteen. It read:

Lady Henrietta Whitfield Conquers Atlantic by Air
The Lady Henrietta Whitfield, the daughter of the late 6th Earl of Hardingham, arrived at her uncle Robert Turnbull's estate in Northumberland today following a direct and nonstop flight from Washington, DC, in the Americas. Her sixty-five-hour flight aboard the airship, christened the *Lady Cimarron*, marks the first transatlantic crossing by air. The ship was constructed by her uncle, the well-known American tycoon Robert Turnbull, who accompanied her. The Lady Henrietta was not just a passenger but in fact served as navigator, guiding the airship on her epic voyage. According to Captain Alexander VonKleist, the passage was unremarkable, aside from being an historic first.

The *Daily Mail* was slightly more excited, putting its story on page eight. It included the fact that American papers had elevated Henrietta's status to that of "Queen of the Sky." Even with that, the story didn't capture the public's imagination. It seemed all of Britain was interested only in news of the war. The general lack of interest in things American was understandable after the full text of President Roosevelt's declaration of American neutrality:

The people of these United States are drawn from many, indeed mostly from, nations now at war. It is to be expected there should be a variety of sympathies and desires among us regarding to the issues and circumstances of this conflict. Some will favor one nation. Some will, no doubt, support another.

But if you love this country of ours above all others, your first loyalty must be to it and to no foreign power.

We as a nation cannot allow ourselves to be drawn into hostile camps, drawn hot against each other. Such division would be fatal to our peace of mind and might seriously stand in the way of the performance of our sacred duty as the one great nation still at peace. We stand as the one people who hold the olive branch, a people who stand ready to play the part of impartial mediator. To fulfill this obligation, we must not become partisan or a participant. We must remain a friend to all.

For this reason, I declare this nation will remain neutral in fact as well as in name during these days that are to try men's souls. We will be impartial in thought as well as action, put a curb upon our sentiments and upon transactions that might be construed as a preference of one party to the struggle before another. To do less will make it more difficult rather than less difficult to resolve that which divides the world.

Her most recent trip to America had given Henrietta time to think about home. She decided she'd been a little harsh on Mommy. All her mother wanted was the best for her daughter, even if she wasn't good at parenting. Henrietta resolved to let bygones be bygones.

That first night, Henrietta had introduced her crewmates. "Mother, let me introduce my captain, Alexander VonKleist, and his wife, Margaretha." Turning to Sebastian, she added, "And this is Mr. Cooke."

Lady Hardingham was so pleased that at last Henrietta had called her Mother, she forgot herself. She stepped forward and hugged her daughter. "Oh, Henriette…you've always called me Mommy." Composing herself, she added, "I am so pleased to meet all of you. Welcome to England and my home. You all must stay here as my guests." The entire crew was grateful. They and their ship needed a rest.

Uncle Robert dragged the work crew away from Ruxmour Manor and put them to work building a barracks for the men. Constructed a short distance from the hangar, it was spacious. The barracks boasted the latest in electric lights and indoor plumbing. A mess hall was attached with a full staff of cooks together with a massive and well-stocked pantry. Uncle Robert even provided several steam-powered automobiles so that the men could visit the pub in the nearby town.

Beatrice made arrangements at Ruxmour Manor for Uncle Robert, Henrietta, Alexander, Margaretha, and Sebastian. Uncle Robert invited several others. Given the number of guests, Beatrice retained additional staff, including two lady's maids and a half-dozen others. They were crowded and cramped into the uncompleted servants' quarters.

When Henrietta first moved to England when she was a teenager, she'd had a difficult time with the rigid class distinctions between her parents and the household staff. Over the years, she'd gotten used to it but resolved that if she were ever in charge of a house, that would change. Even so, she'd enjoyed having someone help her dress. It would be a relief and not a burden to have the help of a lady's maid once again.

For Margaretha, the experience was all new and a bit confusing. When Henrietta told her about what was planned and introduced the maid, Margaretha sputtered, "A lady's maid? What am I supposed to do with a lady's maid?"

Henrietta giggled. "Enjoy it."

"How? You've enjoyed that kind luxury all your life. I haven't. This woman knows more about how a lady behaves than I do. I should be working for her."

Henrietta took both of Margaretha's hands. "You remember when I said you were coming along on the *Lady Cimarron*? Then you had to teach me everything except navigation? We'll just consider this part of your reward."

"Reward! But—"

Then, pointing to the badges on her collar, Henrietta barked, "Flight Lieutenant, you are going to learn how to behave as a proper lady, like it or not, so get used to it. That is an order. Do you hear me?" At that, they both broke into the giggles.

With the *Lady Cimarron* safely in its hangar at Ruxmour, Henrietta had little to do. Officially, the examination and repair of the *Lady Cimarron* was to be left to the ground crew, who had arrived from America. Uncle Robert had dispatched them before the *Lady Cimarron* departed from St. Louis. They were already at sea when the *Cimarron* arrived in Washington. Even so, Henrietta refused "to be left out of the fun of going over every inch of the *Lady Cimarron*."

While Captain VonKleist told the press the trip across the Atlantic had been unremarkable, implying it was routine, he hadn't been completely truthful. The reality was there had been some harrowing moments. The second night out, still a thousand miles from Europe, the problem occurred. Henrietta was on the bridge as officer of the watch. The weather had been bad earlier but was clearing rapidly. The ship was still bumping up and down but not violently. Captain VonKleist had been up for two days straight. Exhausted, he'd gone to his cabin to take a short nap, leaving the Queen of the Sky in charge. He and Margaretha were still in their cabin, and Sebastian, while not on duty, tried to sit in the first officer's seat to help Henrietta stay awake. He failed, so Henrietta ordered him off the bridge. He was now asleep in his bunk.

During the storm, one of the smart bombs worked itself partly loose and began to swing freely. It damaged the cargo-handling mechanism. Trapped in the hold, it armed itself and threatened to blow the ship apart. Henrietta was very conscious of the ship, and when the slight vibration began, she sent Flight Officer Theodore Pierce to investigate. He was younger than Henrietta, in fact the youngest man aboard, and his baby face made him look like a teenager. She had taken him on as her most junior "navigator-in-training." Now he sat with her, seeking guidance on a navigation problem she had assigned to him.

Pierce returned ashen faced. Henrietta didn't hesitate. Turning to the senior flight lieutenant on the bridge, she said, "Props, ahead slow. Helm, keep us steady. Flight, Mr. Jamison, you have the con. I need to take a look at this!" Henrietta disappeared up the ship's ladder into the ship. From behind her, she heard a chorus of "aye!"s. She heard Flight the loudest, who was saying, "I have the con, aye."

Henrietta ran to the rear hold. The bomb was hanging by a single attachment point. They could see the safety pin with its red ribbon was missing, and the bomb was armed. The terrified young crewman blurted, "The hatch cover is broken, jammed half closed! We can't drop it! If it falls, it will explode, and... " Shaking with fear, he continued, "...and we'll all die."

Henrietta outwardly appeared calm. Inside her chest, her heart pounded, threatening to explode. She tried to coolly assess the situation. In as steady a voice as she could manage, she said, "Mr. Pierce, get a grip on yourself. We'll just tie it off, and it will not be a problem."

"But we're a thousand feet in the air, and whoever tries will fall..."

"Please calm down. Get me a line, and I'll do it." He hesitated, so Henrietta softly and calmly added, "Quickly, if you please, Mr. Pierce, and be quiet. We don't want to wake the others over something little like this."

The young man was so shaken, he couldn't answer. He nodded and ran. A moment later, he reappeared with a rope. Henrietta directed him, "Secure the end, and then be ready to pull when I tell you."

"Then what?"

"Then I will climb down on what is left of the hatch cover, disarm the bomb, and tie it off."

"But—"

"No buts. You are in no condition to do it." Henrietta grabbed the line, looped it, and slung it over her shoulder. Then, grabbing the frame, she stepped out into space. "One hand for the ship, one for you," she repeated as she worked her way out. She thought of the monkeys she'd admired in the London Zoo. She mumbled, "If only I had a tail."

The frame to the hatch cover was not intended to carry a man's weight. Henrietta hoped it would hold her. She inched farther and farther into the darkness. As she did, she could feel the frame sag and threaten to give way. She thought to herself, "If it fails and I fall, I will hold on no matter what. Maybe I can pull it with me far enough to let the bomb drop."

The frame moaned but held. She cautiously continued forward. Her foot slipped twice, but she recovered. When she was in place, she pulled a hair stick from her chignon. Her hair fell. As the wind caught it, she paused to push it out of her face. Holding herself by one hand, she stretched out and barely reached the bomb with the other. Gingerly, she inserted the stick as a replacement for the missing safety pin. She pulled back, took a breath, and changed hands. Pulling the loop from her shoulder, she slid it over the end of the bomb.

She looked up. By this time, Sebastian and several crewmen had joined Mr. Pierce. "Gentlemen, if you would be so kind, please pull." The bomb inched upward. When it was clear enough, a heavier rope was looped and handed down. Henrietta pushed it into place. She said, "Go ahead and pull it up." The crewmen strained, and the bomb inched upward. In minutes, it was reattached to the bomb rack. Henrietta eased her way back.

The crew cheered. Sebastian forgot himself and grabbed her in a hug. "Henrietta, you could have been killed!"

Henrietta pulled back. "As you were, Mr. Cooke! Gentlemen, please, you'll wake the others."

It was too late. The whole crew was up and abuzz. As Henrietta made her way down the ladder, she was greeted by Alexander. "What were you thinking?! You could have fallen!"

"I was thinking of the ship. As an officer, my first duty is to her." Pushing past him, she added, "Captain, if you can spare me for a few minutes, I am afraid the wind has taken my hair, and I'll need a short time to make myself presentable."

Alexander smiled. "Please take all the time you need. I have the con."

"Thank you, Captain. Margaretha, if I could trouble you, I'll need a bit of help. Will you please join me in my cabin?"

Then, as outwardly calm as a still pond on a summer day, she turned and walked to her cabin. Margaretha followed her in and closed the door.

Henrietta collapsed on the seat. The adrenaline gone, she began to shake. "Margaretha, I was so scared. I…I could have fallen, and…"

Margaretha sat beside her. Giving her a hug, she said, "Oh, you brave, brave, girl. Everything is fine now. You are safe. Thanks to you, we all are safe."

Henrietta wanted to cry but held back her tears and hung on. They sat quietly until there was a knock at the door. Henrietta sat up. "Enter.

It was Mr. Pierce. "My lady, I thought you might like a cup of tea."

"Thank you, Mr. Pierce. You are very thoughtful. As you can see, we are not quite finished here, but if you will be so kind as to inform the captain, I will be back at my station in ten minutes."

"Ten minutes. Yes, my lady."

That is how it started. Mr. Pierce made it a point to call her by her title from then on. If every crewman hadn't already respected her, this event made them feel they owed her their lives. By the end of the next day, all but the most senior officers had begun following Mr. Pierce's example. Thereafter, she was always addressed as "my lady."

By morning light, a crewman wearing an improvised harness got the hatch cover fixed, closed, and secured. When the *Lady Cimarron* arrived in England, nothing appeared amiss.

Uncle Robert had experience dealing with the press. Taking a lead from his friend President Roosevelt, Robert contacted the editors and publishers of the British newspapers so they could cover the story when the *Lady Cimarron* landed. He invited them to send a representative to join a small group of

American reporters who were planning to be his guests at Ruxmour. More correctly, they were staying at a hotel, the Ruxmour Arms, he owned a short distance away. The war had drawn off nearly all of the senior and most experienced men in the British press, but the newspapers felt obliged to send someone. They sent eager freelancers and stringers to cover the arrival. Most were either just getting started in the business or had other limitations preventing them from relocating to London or running off to the continent. Among them were reporters from the local papers in Edinburgh, Glasgow, and Leeds; a sport reporter from Manchester; a one-legged former war correspondent living on a pension; and two young ladies more interested in having a career than a family.

Uncle Robert talked to each as they arrived, and he made two things clear. First was that his niece Henrietta was a proper English lady and would at all times be treated as such; salacious gossip and false stories about her would get them run off the property. Second, if they behaved like ladies and gentlemen, each would be rewarded with a tour of the *Lady Cimarron* and a chance to interview Henrietta and several other members of the crew. It was a fair bargain. Henrietta herself accompanied each tour and spoke with the reporters. They wrote their stories and filed them, but the war news consumed the papers. Those stories that were published were short and inoffensive.

The captain ordered the crew to remain silent when it came to the story of the bomb. Under no circumstances was it to be mentioned to the press. The reason was very simple. No one was to know the *Lady Cimarron* had come to Britain as a warship as well as a passenger liner. It would take several weeks to fabricate a new set of bomb racks and have them installed. Modifications to the hangar doors also took quite some time.

Uncle Robert had also ordered a special modification to the ship at the request of the admiralty. Sebastian, on Robert's behalf, explained it to Henrietta. "We're modifying the forward cargo bays by adding platforms on which we can mount cannons."

"Cannons? Won't the recoil damage the ship?"

"No, not at all. They are special Mark III QF six-pounder Hotchkiss guns. We modified them with a better recoil system than was on the old Mark II system introduced back in 1890."

"But it's still a cannon?"

"Yes, just a small one that shoots a shell about two and a quarter inches across and weighs, wait for it...six pounds."

"Ha-ha, very clever!"

"It is really very clever. We have four of them now and more on the way."

Now safely in her mother's residence, Henrietta made herself at home. Her mother had refused to keep horses after her husband's death but did have Henrietta's favorite mount stabled on a nearby estate. With a little encouragement, Henrietta persuaded those who loved to ride to accompany her. Uncle Robert begged off, claiming he was too busy. Alexander was a city boy and really didn't like riding in or on anything without an engine. Sebastian was very busy with a new gas controller. That left Margaretha and Henrietta on their own.

Margaretha loved riding nearly as much as Henrietta did. They and Flight Officer Pierce, who by this time had attached himself to Henrietta as her aide, went riding several times. They even managed to have picnics. When not riding and picnicking, Henrietta spent many hours with Alexander and Sebastian learning the intricacies of controlled flight. She marveled at their intelligence.

It was all very informal, but still she could feel herself growing into something of an expert. Uncle Robert was embroiled in constant negotiations. It seemed that no sooner would one problem be resolved than another would arise. His problems all stemmed from the delays the war created in shipping parts to Britain. The parts were needed to complete another Cimarron. Alexander had assumed responsibility to oversee day-to-day construction operations. What was being actually discussed and the progress of the construction remained secret. Sebastian took charge of seeing to repairs of the *Lady Cimarron*. The only time the girls could pull them away were those evenings when they had a meeting over dinner.

Uncle Robert worked tirelessly trying to get the first of his ships he'd sold to the British completed. He complained, "All of the parts, including engines, are manufactured in the United States and are shipped via Canada. With the war, some of my critical parts, including all but one of the engines, have been delayed."

"Is that a problem?"

"The Royal Navy is anxious to get into the air and start training crews. Without any background in Cimarrons, there is a lot to learn and very little of it has been written down."

Uncle Robert proposed that volunteers be posted on the *Lady Cimarron* to learn how to operator her. The Royal Navy liked the idea, but the objection of the American ambassador put an end to it. Nevertheless, the Royal Navy pushed ahead in establishing a training and gunnery school just fifteen miles from Ruxmour. It helped that at least the simulator of the bridge had arrived on time. The only real drawback, aside from the delay, was that no one outside of the *Lady Cimarron*'s crew had any actual flight experience.

Several groups of trainees were given tours of the *Lady Cimarron* as she underwent repairs. As each would arrive for the first time, Alexander would take the time needed to greet them. "Gentlemen, welcome to the *Lady Cimarron*. This is a commercial vessel, but we command it much as you might expect a warship to be commanded. We cannot afford to have any miscommunication. Every member of this crew is an officer, and all have earned flight wings. Wings indicate the wearer has completed training and can perform every task necessary to keep this ship airborne. It is more than an honor. In a crisis, they will be in command because they know what is required. This is why we have a rule. In an air emergency, even the most junior flight officer with wings outranks all others aboard.

"Second, I am sure you are aware the Lady Henrietta is our second officer and navigator. Having a woman in a command role aboard ship may seem inappropriate. Let me assure you, in this case it is not. She is as brave and selfless as any man and deserves your respect. I've flown with her in massive storms. Of all of us aboard, she was the most composed. I've witnessed her climb out on a bit of the damaged frame a thousand feet up in the darkness and over the open hold and disarm a bomb with her hair stick. She was as cool as a cat. Whatever else you might think about her, know that if there is a problem, she will keep her head. It is why she is always addressed as 'my lady' by the crew. Questions?"

There were many questions but none about the wisdom of having the lady aboard. She clearly had earned the right to be there. To a man, the naval officers were impressed by her calm command demeanor and the knowledge she obviously possessed about the ship. When over dinner Mr. Pierce suggested that one day in the not-too-distant future the lady might be captain of her own ship, none disagreed. She indeed was a woman to be taken seriously.

Chapter Seven:
News from the Front

Every morning, the newspapers were filled with accounts of French forces suffering another disastrous defeat. The Schlieffen Plan, on which the Germans depended, was flawed, requiring the advance to be uninterrupted and the conquest complete in only forty-two days. It failed to make adequate provision to move the massive number of troops needed or to resupply them once they arrived. If there was any interruption in road or rail service, it would fail. These flaws were of great concern to the German General Staff, but they all proved to be inconsequential. German airships made all the difference. They allowed the Germans to track enemy movements from the air, make precision bombing raids, and focus ground attacks on weak points. The subsequent advances were so rapid that roads, bridges, and most importantly railroads were captured almost completely intact.

On the morning of the sixth day, with German forces deep into Belgium, the fortresses at Namur fell, and the Belgians were forced into a headlong retreat toward Antwerp. They remained an effective force until King Leopold was killed during a raid by German airships. The crown fell to his twenty-eight-year-old younger brother, Albert, who immediately attempted to rally his troops, only to be killed the following day. The loss of their kings took the fight out of many, who began spreading wild rumors, and panic ensued. On the eighth day, with the German forces shelling Antwerp, the Belgians sued for peace. The collapse of the Belgians occurred so quickly, their railroad infrastructure survived and fell into German hands. Across the border, large segments of French railroads in the extreme northeast of the country were also captured before defenders knew the enemy was upon them.

When Henrietta came in for breakfast, she found Uncle Robert sitting at the table reading the morning paper. "Good morning, Uncle. Anything of interest in the paper?"

Uncle Robert just shook his head. "I cannot believe it. The Belgians gave up, and the Germans are going after what's left of the French army."

"How can that be? The war is only a week old."

"Eight days, but it is true, and according to what's in the paper, the railroads in Belgium are still running and shuffling German troops forward."

"Can the French hold on?"

"I don't know. From what it says here, it is a race, and the French are losing."

As bad as the newspaper reports were, the situation on the ground was actually far worse. The Germans had refocused their energies on the remaining French army and began their push toward the fortress of Maubeuge, France. The power of the German onslaught was irresistible. The horrific bombardment from the air terrified the army and the populace alike. French forces abandoned their positions and ran for their lives every time an airship appeared.

It wasn't just the bombs. With aerial spotting, the German artillery was particularly effective. The ruined fortresses at Maubeuge and the city fell on the thirteenth day of fighting. French fixation at the beginning of the war on attempts to recover Alsace-Lorraine made matters for them much worse than might otherwise have been expected. Much of their army was sent too far south and east to defend Paris and the heartland.

The ever-efficient German Staff had anticipated the French would try to redeploy their forces. A covering German force slowed the French advance into Germany until matters in the west brought the need to redeploy the army. The judicious bombing of key bridges and rail facilities did not stop the French redeployment but so disrupted the effort that the movement of French troops became like that of a disorganized mob trying to push through a quagmire. The result was that the French were outnumbered in every engagement.

The situation at Ruxmour developed into a routine. Every morning, Uncle Robert would read the paper and then share news of the latest disaster over breakfast. When he announced on the twelfth day of fighting, "The first elements of the British Expeditionary Force arrive in La Havre. Now the Germans are going to see what our professional army can do against a bunch of conscripts." The next day's paper brought bad news. The first few ships loaded with troops were mercilessly bombed from the air with great loss of life. The effort to land troops continued, and by the time Maubeuge fell, some eighty thousand British troops were in France. They confronted the chaos. The disorganized French forces planned to make a stand east of Amiens.

On learning the British Army was in the field, the kaiser ordered his army to destroy "those contemptible English fools." The German 1st Army drove west along the channel while the 2nd Army drove straight at the city. The British commander of the expeditionary force proved to be the very embodiment of British military incompetence. General Neville Waterford-Smyth issued a series of confused and conflicting orders. Initial encounters by individual British units were highly successful, but the lack of proper coordination doomed the enterprise and resulted in several lost opportunities.

The situation rapidly deteriorated. With nothing of substance to stop them, German cavalry forces arrived to the northwest of Armies, France, on the evening of the twenty-second day of the war. The morning brought a bigger disaster. In three weeks, the German army had crossed the River Somme and threatened to envelop the entire British force. The general, without consulting his French counterparts, first ordered a withdrawal of British forces toward Dieppe; then, discovering it lacked a true deep-water port for evacuation, he panicked and ordered the force to Le Havre. This unanticipated move divided the French and British armies. The Germans, having command of the air, discovered the development at once. They fell upon the unprepared left flank of the French army. It was a rout. The way to Paris was now open.

Events spun wildly out of control. The French government fell, and the new prime minister vowed to fight on. The next day, the Germans detected a gap in the French line east of Paris at Mary-sur-Marne. In their rush to defend the capital from the German threat from the north and west, French units lost contact with each other. Believing trailing units were right behind them, the lead elements pushed on. A combination of air strikes and artillery slowed the trailing units to a stop. A gap of nearly twenty miles opened. It was an open invitation to the Germans, who, in a furious all-day attack, destroyed the French screening force and then crossed the Marne and turned west. The Germans were less than forty miles from the heart of Paris.

The French government fell again. The new prime minister, after urging every Frenchman to fight for the city to the bitter end, was caught by an angry crowd as he attempted to flee the capital by automobile. It did not end well, and he was assassinated. By morning, France had its third new government in as many days. The army now turned to make a stand, but a series of massive air raids and unending artillery fire doomed the effort.

On the thirty-fifth day of the war, the Germans broke through the line and were poised to take Paris by storm. The German commander threated to raze the city unless the war ended. The French government decided France had suffered enough and asked for armistice. In five weeks, the Germans had conquered their biggest rival.

Uncle Robert reassured Henrietta, "The German victories are troubling, but Britain is hardly in the desperate situation France was in. The battleships of the Royal Navy outnumber the Germans' five to one. Behind the steel wall of ships, this island nation is invulnerable."

At Ruxmour, it was hard to believe there was a war going on. Henrietta found that she had become quite popular and received letters from people she hadn't heard from in years. With the exception of one short note to a childhood friend just back from university, she left the letters unanswered. That was until her mother found out. Beatrice forced her daughter to respond to many of them. It was a chore, but it was something to do on rainy days until the airship was repaired. On sunny days, she would spend hours staring up at the clouds. *There is where my home is now*, she would say over and over to herself.

The war news continued to be bad. In the early days, there was good news from the Russian front. Its army moved surprisingly quickly against the Austro-Hungarians and invaded Galica almost immediately after hostilities had begun. Austro-Hungary, having feared this Russian invasion, sent the largest part of its army north to resist. The Russians soundly defeated the ill-led Austro-Hungarian forces and sent them in a headlong retreat.

Simultaneously, the Hapsburg army attempted to invade Serbia, which was an even bigger disaster. It failed on the same day France lost Amiens. Emperor Franz Joseph's army was forced to retreat. The losses on the battlefields rekindled independence movements throughout the non-German-speaking parts of the empire. Hungary declared itself independent, and a civil war broke out. Emperor Franz Joseph asked the kaiser for help, but there was none to give. The German army had its hands full in France.

The Austro-Hungarian Empire fell into a revolutionary death spiral. The emperor, while personally loved and respected, led the most autocratic government outside of Russia. It made him the target. The strain of losing his son to suicide, his wife to assassination, and his empire to revolution proved too much for the seventy-five-year monarch, and he suffered a heart attack. His successor, Franz Ferdinand, was rumored to be insane and inspired no confidence.

What was unknown at the time was that a second Russian army was preparing to march into East Prussia on the morning of the twenty-first day of the war. As the army massed, the tsar received word of the growing debacle in France. The fall of the fortress at Maubeuge after only two weeks came as a shock. In a remarkable show of restraint by the autocrat, the tsar ordered his army to delay the invasion to the twenty-seventh day of the war. His caution was based on several factors. Russia had been in the throes of a recession for several years leading up to the war. There was growing discontent. Domestic problems were compounded by the Russian struggle with the Japanese in the Far East. War had drained the national will and emptied the treasury. Numerous strikes and riots were a precursor of a full-blown revolution that was imminent. With Austro-Hungary now at war with itself, the discontented pushed for changes within Russia. A growing number of shrill voices called for a full revolution. News of the French rout at Amiens and the British withdrawal prompted a further delay in the planned invasion of Germany, first to the thirty-fifth and then to the thirty-eighth day of the war.

Before a single shot had been fired on the Russo-Prussian front, the French sued for peace, and the tsar found himself facing the might of the German army. The tsar knew that with the French no longer fighting and the British fleeing the continent, his forces would face an overwhelming foe. He knew a defeat like that in France would end his reign. He avoided this by making his own peace with the kaiser.

The tsar was fundamentally an autocrat. He believed in absolute monarchy. Had he had his way, nothing would have changed, but he was not a fool. He could see for himself that the world was changing. He needed to quickly address the growing discontent fueling the revolution. He looked out at Europe. Constitutional monarchs in Britain and Germany were thriving. The autocratic regime in Vienna had collapsed, and the emperor had been forced to abdicate and run for his life. In earlier days, the French had beheaded their king.

It didn't take a genius to see what had to be done if the Russian crown was to survive. The tsar reached out to trusted advisors, including Sergei Witte. He agreed to freedom of assembly, freedom of the press, and the creation of an elected assembly called the Duma. The reforms converted Russia into a constitutional monarchy. The political changes were important, but the real reforms that made a difference were economic. In the cities, the rights of workers to unionize, collectively bargain, and strike were recognized. At the same time, several hated monopolies were broken up.

In the countryside, there was real land reform. Under the previous tsar, Alexander II, land reform had been promised to the serfs. It failed because only the poorest agricultural land was turned over. The imperial family retained nearly one-third of all agricultural land. More to point, the royal family and other elitists kept one hundred percent of the good land. Nicholas, rather than have it taken from him, "gave away" a significant portion of the imperial family's land to the serfs. In fact, the land was permanently leased. It was sold in exchange for a promise of perpetual annual payment. The payment was modest but was indexed to inflation. This gave the tsar the advantage of a secure income stream while undercutting the revolutionaries' biggest complaints.

The Russian ship of state righted itself, and Nicholas went from an unloved pariah to Nicholas the Great in the minds of the Russian people. Backing away from the brink of disaster, the Russian Empire began to renew its strength. Government leaders in London and Tokyo were alarmed. A revitalized Russia that returned to an aggressive policy of expansion was a serious threat. In Berlin, the developments in the east were viewed as a nightmare of epic proportions.

A young firebrand politician and friend of Uncle Robert by the name of Churchill visited Ruxmour on a regular basis. The visits gave him a chance to see the progress being made on building a proper British *Cimarron* fleet. One evening he complained over dinner, "The capitulation by both the French and the Russians leaves us standing alone against the Germans."

Henrietta asked, "If it is all over, will the kaiser pull his army out of Belgium?"

"He hasn't yet. He's holding on right now and making noises like he wants to make it part of the greater German Empire."

Henrietta followed up, asking, "Is that because of the success of his airship campaign?"

"Yes, he thinks he can do whatever he likes. He even believes this is his opportunity to end Britain's dominance in world events, a time for 'his Germany' to take its rightful place as first among the nations of earth."

Chapter Eight:
The Armada

Only three weeks after the fall of France, the kaiser ordered his fleet of airships to attack the Royal Navy. A cruiser squadron was its target as it moved from its base at Portsmouth north to the anchorage at Rosyth in the Firth of Forth. The kaiser learned of the movement thanks to Irish Republicans who wished to see Great Britain lose the war.

Armed with a sailing schedule, the German airships intercepted the force fifty miles due east of Ramsgate shortly after two in the afternoon. The Royal Navy had believed ships moving at sea would be safe from attack despite reports that the *Lady Cimarron* had accomplished the feat off the Virginia coast. The Germans had anticipated this and armed themselves with a new weapon similar to the one Uncle Robert had developed. In total, six heavy cruisers and nine light cruisers were attacked with the loss of all but two of the heavy cruisers and a single light cruiser.

Because all of the fighting had taken place at sea, the attack and the fearful losses had not yet been reported in the press. The government, fearing bad news from the continent could cause problems at home, strictly enforced censorship laws. Every story of action by British forces had to be reviewed and approved before being printed. Failure to abide by this rule was a violation of the Official Secrets Act of 1889 and subjected the publisher and his employees to imprisonment for five years to life. The attack on Portsmouth Squadron was to remain hidden from the public for the time being.

The ballroom was resplendent. Henrietta was elegant in her off-the-shoulder sky-blue silk multilayer ball gown. It was bedazzled with tiny hand-sewn crystals to catch the light as she waltzed. The tight-corseted bodice and petticoats were intended to give the gown the illusion of a hoop skirt of a by-gone era whenever she spun on the dance floor. Her hair was pulled up and topped with a dazzling diamond tiara given to her by Uncle Robert as a token of appreciation for saving the *Lady Cimarron*. In a word, she was stunning.

Henrietta appeared at the top of the stairs with her uncle. He paused so she could descend unaccompanied, as though floating down to the ballroom floor. Remembering how she'd fallen during her first time on the *Lady Cimarron*, she was ever so grateful to her mother, who had insisted Henrietta take dancing lessons and learn how to descend a staircase without falling on her face. Every head in the room turned and stared. She'd lived up to the press reports. She was the very image of the Queen of the Sky. At the foot of the stairs, she stopped until her uncle joined her. Like a proud father of the bride, he walked her straight across the dance floor to make her introduction to their hosts.

The duke had recently returned home after being in India for some years and falling ill. Though he was no longer the robust gentleman Henrietta remembered from her youth, he still had the same mischievous glint in his eyes. Before Uncle Robert could speak, their host spoke first. "Henrietta, I am so glad to see you again."

"Thank you, Your Grace," she said as she blushed at the informality.

"I was sorry to hear of your father's passing. I was away in India. We had such a time together when we were young. I am happy to see you have landed, so to speak, on your feet." Turning to Uncle Robert, the duke said, "Robert, when you said you were going to introduce your niece, you didn't tell me she was our Henrietta."

Robert smiled. "It didn't seem to be important at the time. How was I to know you already knew her or that one day she'd be the Queen of the Sky?"

Henrietta's blush deepened as the two men laughed. Then, with a smirk, their host added to her embarrassment by saying, "As the American press has bestowed the title, who am I to contest it? Your Royal Highness, I am sorry to say I am not the man I once was, so I no longer dance, but you could still make this old man very happy if you'd dance with my son."

The young man at the duke's elbow bowed. Taking a cue from his father, he considered adding, "Your Majesty." Instead, he simply smiled and winked.

Henrietta felt a giggle coming on, so she extended her hand and said, "Anything to get me away from you wicked old men who like to make fun of a helpless young woman."

Henrietta realized she knew the young man. He was the duke's oldest son and was officially the Marquis of Cheviot, but his given name was Coinneach. They'd know each other since they were children. They met when Henrietta was barely thirteen and first learning how to be British. Given her American attitude and boyish interests, he'd teased her, calling her, "Henry" and spelling her name "Henri." If she was to have a boy's name, it seemed only fair he would have a girl's, so she began calling him "Connie."

They had been very close friends as kids, and a harmless teenage romance had begun but ended when Connie's father dragged him off to the subcontinent. They promised to stay in touch and continued to write for a time but all too soon they stopped and lost track of one another. Before they stopped Connie penned the love letters Henrietta held so dearly.

Standing for a long moment she starred. Then fearing she must look like a deer caught in a headlamp Henrietta took a breath. Smiling she looked Connie over. He had grown into a very as handsome a man and on the surface looked every bit the man of her dreams. Connie looked at her, but she could not tell from his expression what he was thinking. He broke what was becoming an awkward silence by gesturing towards the dance floor and saying: "shall we?" Henrietta nodded then took his arm.

As they walked, Henrietta composed herself. The real flesh and blood Connie was beside her. He was no longer just a figment of her imagination. It dawned on her, despite his outward appearance, she really didn't know the man inside. He might be and probably was far different from her fantasy of him. She would have to be careful and not confuse the two. Taking a deep breath, she began: "Lord Cheviot, thank you for saving me."

"Think nothing of it, Henri."

Henrietta smiled. "No one has called me that forever."

"I beg your pardon. I suppose that given what I've read in the press, I really should call you Your Majesty."

"Oh my, I know those silly newspapermen in America called me the Queen of the Sky. Please tell me they haven't started that foolishness here at home."

"I am afraid even the *Times*—"

"Well, don't you start. Please, if you must make fun of me, just stick to calling me Henri."

Coinneach, ashamed, grimaced. "I do so hope I didn't offend you and that we are still friends."

"We are friends even if you tease me. I do appreciate being rescued."

"Then, Henri, you should call me Connie like you used to."

Henrietta was still giggling when they reached the dance floor, just as her favorite Viennese waltz was about to begin. Connie took her hand, the waltz began, and around the room they whirled.

As they danced, Henrietta saw out of the corner of her eye a flash of blonde hair and knew that Margaretha had already dragged poor Alexander onto the floor. She tried to teach him to dance and calculated that if luck was with her, she would be stepped on only four or five times before the dance ended. Sebastian had been enticed to join Uncle Robert and the duke.

When the waltz ended, Connie said, "You dance divinely…not at all like the awkward little girl I remember. I hope you'll save another dance for me."

"It would be honor."

The break in the music was an opportunity to sip a little champagne and give Alexander the opening needed. He stepped forward and addressed young Lord Cheviot. "Sir, as this beautiful lady's captain, I believe the next dance is mine."

It was back to the dance floor. Alexander was not as good a dancer as Connie, but he did his best and managed not to step on Henrietta's feet. She clearly was the belle of this ball.

Henrietta, as an attractive daughter of an earl, had never been a wallflower or wanting for suitors. She was no stranger to having handsome young men expressing an interest in her. What she now faced was far different. This world was completely made of young, dashing, eligible men, all of whom desired her company. In fact, since her arrival back in Britain, the gossip mills had been hard at work, and it was common knowledge she was heir to her uncle Robert's fortune. She'd received no less than a dozen marriage proposals and many other invitations.

Over the next two hours and between sips of champagne, an earl, two viscounts, a baron, and several others presented themselves to Henrietta as dance partners. There were still many more who awaited a turn. They all did their best to impress her, some with conversation, others with their ability as dancers. She did her best with all of them. It was exhausting. The champagne they continued to foist on her was not helping, that and the memory of the first dance of the evening. She and Connie had been close at one time, and she had missed his company.

The ball dragged on, and Henrietta was approaching the limit of her endurance when Connie showed up again. "You promised me at least one more dance tonight, didn't you?" She'd hoped he'd come and rescue her again. Just to dance with someone who knew how would be a refreshing departure from the ordeal of dancing with those who didn't.

Connie stepped forward. He prepared to sweep Henrietta into his arms and then down the *Blue Danube*.

Henrietta would happily have danced with Connie, but she desperately needed a respite. She took his arm and said, "Would you mind terribly if we were to step outside and let me have a moment to catch my breath?"

Connie returned her smile. "Anything you desire is my command."

They walked from the ballroom through the big doors and out into the garden. From there they would have a clear view of the fireworks that the duke had promised at midnight. The evening air was a delightful reprieve from the heat inside the ballroom, and the aroma of the flowers drifted on the slight breeze. The full moon cast its light from just across the tree line in the distance. Between the music from the ballroom behind them and the light of the moon, it was magical.

Henrietta hung onto Connie's arm, and they strolled out from the house. Screwing his courage to the sticking place, he stopped and faced her. He said, "Henrietta, I'd like to talk to you about something."

She looked up at his face and smiled. The moon illuminated her face. It highlighted the sparkle in her eyes. She waited expectantly. He looked in her eyes and got lost. After a long moment, Henrietta asked, "You said you want to talk?"

"Henrietta, you and I have known each other a long time, and recently I've thought of you often and now with the stories about you in the papers, I haven't been able to keep you out of my mind. I just keep thinking about you and me. You must remember how I used to feel about you…feel about us, I mean." He took a deep breath and then said, "I have something I've been trying to get the courage to ask you all evening."

Henrietta's heart jumped into her throat. What was he about to ask her?

Looking into her eyes, he said, "Henrietta, would you…object very much if…since I didn't get the dance you promised me, I was wondering if you'd object if I were to kiss you?"

With relief, Henrietta's smile broadened, and she replied, "I would object very much if you didn't kiss me."

With that, Connie pulled her tightly to him, and they kissed. He'd kissed her before when they were teenagers, but this was different…better. The fireworks display began in the distance and painted the sky. Caught up in the moment, Henrietta would have been happy to stay there in the moonlight kissing. At that moment it seemed like everything she'd imagined when she read his old letters was coming true.

Sadly, the illusion did not last. The spell was broken when a young naval lieutenant arrived without either of them noticing him. He coughed to announce his presence. Henrietta pulled back from Connie. "Begging your pardon, Lady Henrietta," said the lieutenant.

"Yes?"

"Your uncle Robert asked me to find you. If you would come with me, I can take you to him."

The ball was still going strong. The lieutenant took Henrietta through the house and into the library. He stopped at a closed door, where Sebastian was already waiting. Henrietta asked, "Do you know what is going on?"

"Not a clue."

The lieutenant said, "Please wait here. I'll announce you." He opened the door.

Inside, Uncle Robert and Alexander were seated with a gentleman. They stood as she entered. "Henrietta, Sebastian, come in and join us," said Uncle Robert. "Lord Palmer, allow me to introduce my niece, Lady Henrietta, and Mr. Sebastian Cooke."

"Lady Henrietta, I am charmed to meet you. I have read of you in the American papers. Their description does not do you justice."

"Thank you, Lord Palmer. You are too kind."

"Not at all. Now, your uncle tells me that in addition to your beauty, you are made of sterner stuff. I wish more of the young men I encounter were as strong."

"Sir, you are trying to turn my head."

Lord Palmer laughed. "I suspect if I tried, I would fail." Becoming very serious, he began again. "If I may, let me bring us to the point of this meeting. Mr. Turnbull and I have been talking, and I have a special favor to ask of you on behalf of His Royal Majesty. It concerns both of you, so please sit with us."

Henrietta and Sebastian were a bit confused, so Uncle Robert added, "Lord Palmer is First Lord of the Admiralty."

They sat, and Lord Palmer spoke. "Let me begin by telling you the Germans have used their airships to attack the Royal Navy." Henrietta's smile disappeared as she became deeply concerned. "What you don't know, what no one outside of the navy and the government knows, is that the first attack was devastating. The Royal Navy just this afternoon lost several—more than a dozen—cruisers…in one raid."

"Oh my…"

"Worse than that, the ships were at sea and were hit while at full speed. It seems the Germans have crafted a weapon much like the one you demonstrated off the coast of Virginia." Lord Palmer paused for effect. "As you are well aware, the ships the British government purchased from your uncle are as yet incomplete. We have nothing to meet the Germans with when they return."

He paused again, then continued. "What is more disturbing is a message we received from the continent. It appears the kaiser was so encouraged by his success, he's now promised to destroy London if Britain does not surrender. I received a wire from the Foreign Office as I arrived. There has been an ultimatum issued. It is just like the one the kaiser issued the day before he first bombed Paris. We expect the German airships will begin bombing London tomorrow."

Henrietta was stunned. "What can we do?"

Lord Palmer answered, "As you are aware, the American government has declared its neutrality."

Uncle Robert added, "That means American ships and American crews cannot participate in the fighting without risking jail or even loss of citizenship."

Lord Palmer continued, "That is the reason for this request tonight. If the *Lady Cimarron* were a British airship crewed by Britons, there would be no problem."

Uncle Robert smiled like the proverbial cat who had eaten a canary. "Henrietta, my lawyers in the States and my solicitors over here have come up with an idea. I plan to give you the company, or that part of it that is here in Britain, and the *Lady Cimarron*. Since you are a British subject, it will be a British company and a British airship."

"Is the *Cimarron* to be registered with Lloyd's of London as a British merchantman?"

Uncle Robert shook his head. "I thought of that, but Lloyd's lists only ship-ships."

Lord Palmer answered, "That is very true, but the *Lady Cimarron* is just that. She exceeds the one hundred ton dead weight requirement and is designed to carry passengers and cargo across the sea. I think I can convince the management committee at Lloyd's and the barristers that the *Lady Cimarron* is truly a ship, but that is going to take time we don't have."

Sebastian asked, "So where does that take us?"

Lord Palmer answered, "It takes us to the point where we've had to come up with a very creative way to act and act quickly. The prime minister has spoken to His Majesty. The king agrees we need to act now and has issued a royal warrant to the Cimarron Company to provide Cimarrons and airship services to the Crown."

Henrietta still was uncertain what Lord Palmer was saying, so she asked, "I understand my ship would be British, but what then?"

"Then we have the company arm the *Lady Cimarron* and make her into a warship."

"A warship!"

"Yes. Normally the Royal Navy would simply take a ship that was armed and place it under the command of an experienced captain, but your uncle Robert has convinced me that commanding the *Lady Cimarron* requires special skills. Sadly, we have no one in the Royal Navy who is trained. For that reason, we'll need the Britons among the crew to help us. Mr. Cooke, as senior man, you would be captain."

Sebastian protested. "Lord Palmer, there are so few of us."

Uncle Robert replied, "Enough to start training others. You'll have Mr. Adams, the third watch helmsman; Mr. Jackson, the second watch props; and Mr. Brown and Mr. Jones in the engine rooms, plus several of the ground crew, whom I am sure will volunteer."

"No, sir, I don't think you understand. If we are to take the ship into battle, I will need to be free to keep her aloft. It is my specialty. If she is damaged, I will need to be free to leave the bridge."

"You refuse to serve as captain?"

"That is correct. But all is not lost. We have another senior officer and a Briton among the crew who would make an excellent captain."

"Who?"

"Henrietta, of course."

"Me?!"

"A woman?!"

"A girl?!"

Sebastian grinned. "Yes, but not just any woman—she is as brave as any man. Mr. Turnbull, you know that to be true. Remember the first storm and the bomb?"

Uncle Robert nodded. "Well, yes…"

Lord Palmer, looking puzzled, asked, "What bomb?"

Henrietta replied, "The one that swung loose while I was standing watch one night over the Atlantic."

Uncle Robert explained, "One of our demonstration bombs came loose from its mounting, swung down, and damaged the ship."

Sebastian added, "It was more than that. When it came loose, it armed itself. Henrietta climbed out like a top man in the rigging, disarmed it, and tied it off. She saved us all."

Lord Palmer looked at Henrietta in surprise and said, "Did she, now? It seems I may have underestimated you. But still, a woman commanding a warship…I doubt…"

Henrietta was a bit angered by his remark. Challenge her ability merely because of her gender? The nerve! The tomboy inside her welled up, and she readied herself to tell him off. Then reason took hold. Lord Palmer was, after all, the First Lord of the Admiralty.

Fortified with all the champagne she'd consumed, Henrietta chose her words carefully and said sweetly, "Lord Palmer, I had a very interesting conversation with President Roosevelt. He told me that of all the game he had ever hunted, the mother grizzly bear protecting her young was the most formidable. This land that I call home is threatened. Would you have me stand by, wring my hands, and do nothing? I will not! If the Cimarron Airship Company is to be mine, then the *Lady Cimarron* is my baby. I will not stand by and permit this land to be ravaged or for her to go into danger without me!"

Uncle Robert smiled and chuckled, knowing what was coming, while he said, "Henrietta, be reasonable! Women don't go to war."

Hardening her voice into a command tone, she replied, "I am being reasonable. If Boudicca could lead the Britons in a war against the Romans, I can lead a single ship against the Germans."

Even Lord Palmer had to smile. "Yes, she did, but she was Queen Boudicca, and she lost."

"I am not she. I am the Queen of the Sky, and I have the *Lady Cimarron*. I will not lose."

Lord Palmer turned to Uncle Robert. "I still don't know if Britain is ready for its own Joan of Arc."

Henrietta sputtered: "I am no Joan of Arc. She was an ignorant peasant girl who managed to get herself burned as a witch. I am an experienced flyer; a trained navigator and I have prepared myself for a career in the Royal Navy. It is only the fact that I am a woman that prevented..."

Sebastian interrupted Henrietta before she said something she would regret. He addressed the First Lord. "Sir, meaning no disrespect, I doubt if any member of the crew would volunteer to serve if you force Lady Henrietta off the ship. She gives us all strength, and she is our best chance to do all we can for king and country."

Henrietta concluded pleading her case based on her qualifications was not getting her anywhere. In her half-drunken state, she decided a better approach would be open defiance. "Lord Palmer, if His Majesty wishes the *Lady Cimarron* to fight for Britain, then this lady shall be aboard."

Lord Palmer grimaced. "Perhaps a member of the crew..."

"No sir! I shall be captain, or I shall not accept ownership of the company. If I am forced to take it than I will register the *Lady Cimarron* as an American ship."

Lord Palmer looked to Uncle Robert. "But..."

Uncle Robert shook his head. "Sir, it appears the lady has made up her mind for us. I must side with her. If you want the one lady, then I am afraid you must take them both. Those are my terms."

Lord Palmer was nothing if not a politician. He knew when further struggle was pointless. Now was the time to salvage what he could. "Well then, if that is the way it must be, it shall be. I'm sure the admirals will object, but I am confident the Prime minister, Lord Balfour, will be sympathetic. You may not know this, but his sister-in-law, the Lady Frances Balfour, is the president of the Central Society for Women's Suffrage. Lord Balfour supports women's equality but hasn't made an issue out of it because of the rumors."

"Rumors?"

"That he is involved with a married woman. She is a well-known suffragette, and if it comes out, it will be ruinous to them both and the movement. Anyway, that is unimportant. Henrietta, if you are to be captain, you will need gunners from the Royal Navy. You can have the pick of the group of volunteers who are already in training, but some of them, shall we say, may not be open minded. They may not believe that having a woman as captain is a good idea."

Sebastian came to Henrietta's defense. "Then I will make believers of them. I suspect after they are told the whole truth about the lady known as the Queen of the Sky, they will be delighted she herself will be leading them."

"I hope you are correct. Regardless, I must ask if you are to do this that you be prepared to take flight by morning."

Uncle Robert added, "The First Lord is meeting with the admirals at the Royal Navy anchorage at Rosyth at ten in the morning. By that time, the ship should be airborne and on its way. Then, gentlemen, I believe Mr. Cooke and I need to take our leave, thank our hosts, and return to Ruxmour. We need to make certain all is ready while we still have time."

Uncle Robert and Lord Palmer rose, and Lord Palmer said, "Then, Captain Whitfield, let me congratulate you on your first command and wish you Godspeed."

Uncle Robert, Alexander, and Margaretha all insisted on retuning with Henrietta and Sebastian. Alexander put it bluntly: "Henrietta if you plan to sail off like John Paul Jones and take our ship into harm's way, you will need to get what rest you can tonight. I have a feeling once it starts, you will find there will be very little time for even a nap."

Alexander was correct that Henrietta should try to sleep. To her surprise, the events of the day had left their mark, and she did.

The lady's maid opened the drapes to wake her at seven thirty. Henrietta's first thought was that the events of the night before had been a dream. The she realized with a start that it was no dream! What had she done? Had she really demanded to be the captain of a warship? Sitting up straight, she blurted out, "Oh dear, Miss Morrison, it is so late!"

"My lady, Mr. Cooke instructed us to leave you to sleep as long as we could. He said he is meeting with the naval officers who are joining the crew and would prefer it if you waited until at least eight fifteen before joining him."

"Did he say what he was up to?"

"He said he was going to make believers out of them, I think."

Henrietta sighed. "Oh dear, oh dear....I hope he can make a believer out of me." Henrietta dressed as quickly as she could while gulping down a cup of tea and a biscuit. As she was about to leave, there was a knock on the door.

Margaretha came in carrying Henrietta's jacket. "After we finished last night, I stayed up and fixed it for you."

Henrietta looked at it and started to object. "I can't be captain! I don't know what I was thinking!"

Margaretha cut her off. "Hush that kind of talk. You knew exactly what you were thinking. You've told me over and over a woman can do anything a man can do. Now you're going to get to prove it. You are the captain, and everyone is counting on you. If the others are going to accept you as captain, you must look the part."

Margaretha had replaced the silver collar tabs of a flight leader. Henrietta's black uniform jacket now bore the silver badges of a captain.

Over breakfast, Mr. Cooke met with the naval officers he picked off the list of volunteer trainees. He told them, "I was present when the First Lord of the Admiralty himself appointed the captain. The decision is final. If after you meet the captain you do not think you can accept the decision, you are free to decline to join the crew. The appointment was made at a meeting last night. I know this because I was there."

One of the officers asked, "What is the hurry? We were sent here by automobile in the dark. Has something happened?"

Sebastian answered, "Mr. Roberts, yes, something has. German airships attacked several cruisers off of Ramsgate yesterday. They sank more than a dozen during a running battle. We are told the kaiser promised late yesterday to destroy London if Britain does not surrender. It was the same type of ultimatum he gave the French. We expect the German airships will return to try for London later today. By Royal Warrant signed by the king, His Majesty's Airship *Lady Cimarron* will stop them.

Another officer asked, "When do we meet the captain?"

Sebastian looked at his watch. "Very soon."

Flying Officer Pierce stuck his head in at the back of the room and nodded. Sebastian said sharply, "Attention on deck!"

Everyone snapped to attention, and Henrietta marched in and up to the front of the room. From her long talks with the retired captain who had taught her navigation, she knew what military courtesy demanded.

Addressing the gathering standing, she said, "Gentlemen, be seated. I am your captain. You may address me as 'captain' or 'my lady.' If any of you object to having me as your leader, I suggest you think of Elizabeth, Victoria, and Boudicca. If after that you still have objections, you are free to stay behind. The Germans are already in the air, and I intend to do battle with them today. We lift in thirty minutes. Be aboard, or I will leave you behind."

As Henrietta turned to leave, everyone stood and remained at attention as she marched briskly from the room. When she was gone, Sebastian said, "Gentlemen, she, for your information, is Lady Henrietta Whitfield, and, yes indeed, she is the individual the press calls the Queen of the Sky. My place is with her, so I will leave you to decide who among you will join us."

Every officer knew his duty. If Henrietta was captain of the *Lady Cimarron*, so be it. Battle was imminent. Only a coward would stay behind. Everyone ran to get aboard. At precisely nine, with a full crew, Henrietta gave the order, "Up ship."

Just after the HMA *Lady Cimarron* departed to fight the Germans, Uncle Robert and the First Lord's representative, Captain Honeycutt of the Royal Navy, met with the reporters who had managed to arrive. Uncle Robert began, "Ladies and gentlemen, thank you for joining us this morning. We have news, but before we share it, we must warn you that what you are about to hear is subject to the Secrets Act. You cannot reveal it until you are given permission. Do you all agree?" The reporters nodded. "Then if we are agreed, Captain Honeycutt, you have the floor."

Captain Honeycutt cleared his throat and said, "As you know, yesterday the German kaiser issued an ultimatum to Britain demanding we surrender or he would destroy London. We expect German airships to start bombing later today." A murmur went through the group. "That is not all. Early today, His Majesty's Airship *Lady Cimarron* departed from here and is headed to London. The *Lady Cimarron* has been specially modified to allow it to attack the Germans in the air."

The reporter from Leeds asked, "Is there going to be a battle?"

The captain responded, "Like none other in history—a battle in the sky."

The reporter from Glasgow, ashen faced, asked, "I thought the *Lady Cimarron* was owned by an American, and America is neutral?"

The captain nodded. "America is neutral, but HMA *Lady Cimarron* is British. She—and in fact the entire Cimarron Airship Company of Great Britain—is owned by Lady Henrietta Whitfield. Lady Henrietta is a subject of the crown, so the *Lady Cimarron* is a British airship, and I might add, has an all-British captain and crew."

The female reporter named Bonnie Winston asked, "But who? Captain VonKleist is an American, isn't he?"

Uncle Robert answered. "Bonnie, I'm glad you asked. Captain VonKleist is definitely American, but he is not aboard." Bonnie looked confused. Uncle Robert continued, "Lady Henrietta is British. She is the owner and now the captain."

The reporter from Edinburgh was shocked. "A woman!"

"A lady," said Robert, "and, as your paper so aptly put it, the Queen of the Sky." That brought stunned silence to the room.

Captain Honeycutt continued. "The Germans do not expect that HMA *Lady Cimarron* can or will attack. It will come as a great surprise to them. However, once battle is joined, it will no longer be secret. At that point, you will be free to send your stories and spread the news."

Uncle Robert added, "All of this is going to break like a monstrous thunderclap. You can expect your editors will all demand stories from you. We've made special arrangements to transmit them to your papers. In fairness, we'll draw lots to see the order for using the telegraph. The system is limited to about two hundred words a minute. If you can keep the first stories short, two hundred words or less, you'll keep all your editors happy and give them what they need. A little later, you all may file much longer stories."

Aboard HMA *Lady Cimarron*, the crew began to settle in. At the suggestion of the Royal Navy, the bomb-aiming equipment had been replaced. The area was now a dedicated plotting room to help track the multiple targets they would be facing. The partition between the station and the bridge had been removed. The station would be gunnery, or guns. Henrietta asked the senior naval officer on board, Lieutenant Commander Reginald Wilkinson, to stay with her on the bridge. When they had first met, she had taken an instant liking to him. She considered naming him the gunnery officer. After thinking it through, she had a better idea. "Mr. Wilkinson, as this will be the first air battle in history, I would like you to make best use of all of our guns."

"Certainly, captain. It would be my honor to serve as gunnery officer, but my place is with my gun crew."

"I understand, and I would not ask, but as you are the senior regular Navy man aboard, you are far more familiar with the guns than I. Our best hope for success lies with your making our shots count."

Mr. Wilkinson agreed. He admired the captain's willingness to both recognize the need for help and ask for it. Still, he looked a little disappointed that he himself would not be allowed to fire a gun at the enemy. Seeing this, the captain added, "Please consider this a promotion. It is the duty of the first officer to do as her captain requests and remain at her side during action."

Mr. Wilkinson brightened. "First officer! Yes, captain. Thank you. Thank you, my lady." He paused. "I just assumed Mr. Cooke would be…"

"I need Mr. Cooke to keep the ship in the air. It is his specialty."

From his station at flight, Sebastian added, "Mr. Wilkinson, I can assure you, I have more than enough to do already. I believe it is best for us all for me to remain here. Congratulations!"

Henrietta then said, "It is settled. Mr. Wilkinson, my friend, we shall fight the ship together."

The *Lady Cimarron* flew south at flank speed. In four hours, the River Thames was visible. A stream of wireless messages told of the location of the German air armada. During the flight, Henrietta took the time to go to each member of the crew and speak to them individually. She wanted everyone to understand what was at stake and what she and they were expected to do. She considered using the words of Shakespeare's Richard III but decided it would be a bit much. Instead, she copied the example of Henry V, moving among the crew, calling them her brothers and cheering them up. It was a "little touch of Henrietta." Her words were, "Whatever may occur after today, should we survive, I will always consider you my brothers." Then with a smile, she would then add, "If you wouldn't consider me too bold, I'll ask you to permit your sister to bestow a kiss on you, just for luck."

Most were happy with a kiss on their cheek or forehead. One junior member of the gun crew, a rather forward and rakishly handsome sublieutenant named Michael Jamison, stole a kiss from her on the lips. Far from offending his captain, it made her giggle. Henrietta smiled and told him, "Well done, Mr. Jamison. I am delighted to see at least one man aboard has the courage to seize the day. I expect great things from you." Sensing the others might become jealous, she smiled and said, "If we come through this together, I will owe each of you a kiss of your own." Several vowed it was a prize worth dying for.

Henrietta also took the time to speak to Sebastian privately in her cabin. She began, "Sebastian, about last night…I just wanted to say—"

Sebastian smiled. "It was wonderful."

"It was, the music and the champagne were wonderful but please don't make too much of it."

"Oh, I thought it was something—"

"It was something, but…I don't know what I was thinking when I insisted I be captain."

"Henrietta, I talked to Alexander and Margaretha. I agree with them. The Germans bombed Antwerp and Paris. You know they've killed who knows how many. Now they threaten everyone and everything you hold dear. You did the only thing you could do—you volunteered. Right now, Britain needs you. We all need you."

Sebastian reached for Henrietta. "I know that now isn't the best time, but it may be my only chance to tell you how special you are and that…I need you."

Henrietta stepped back, staring at Sebastian. "No, please don't. It's not that way between us. It can't be that way. I like you, but…but Sebastian, it's just...we are crewmates…shipmates who shared an adventure, but it was as friends."

Sebastian tried again. "I thought maybe we could be more than just friends."

"Sebastian, don't say things like that. You are one of my dearest friends, and I now need your help as a friend."

Crestfallen, Sebastian moved back. "I understand. You are the captain, and I'm just…"

Henrietta knew she needed to say something, so she said the first thing that came to mind. "No, Sebastian, it is not you.... There is someone else..." As she said it, she realized that if he asked who it was, she didn't have an answer. There was no one except the man she'd imagined from the love letters. She simply couldn't tell Sebastian about him without sounding like a foolish girl. To prevent being caught in a lie, or worse yet being found out, she let her voice trail off.

Henrietta's declaration caught Sebastian off guard. "Oh, I didn't know.... I mean, you've never mentioned anyone, and I assumed...I apologize."

Relieved she was not going to be embarrassed, Henrietta replied, "No need for that."

Sebastian straightened his back and offered her his hand. "Still friends?"

"Friends to the end and forever."

They returned to the bridge as though nothing had happened.

At a quarter past one, the Germans were spotted on the horizon just off the port quarter of the bow. Henrietta's stomach knotted, but she gripped the armrest of her command chair and said softly, "So, Mr. Wilkinson, tell me; what do you make of them?"

Using his binoculars, he studied the sky. "The wireless said they were making a show of force. Reports are they are flying in V formations like birds. They're stretched out across the sky for miles."

"That's the same formation they used when they first bombed Paris, isn't it?"

"Yes. This time it looks like they've pulled together most everything they have. Over Paris, they had twenty-eight. Last report is this time it is five groups of seven for a total of thirty-five. The leader seems to be using the Thames to navigate. At this distance, I can make out only three—no, four, five, six, seven."

Guns added, "That's just the first wave. I can make out a second wave behind them."

Henrietta's knuckles turned white. She said to her first officer, "As we close, give me a bearing. I intend to place this ship where she will do them the most harm."

Henrietta and the others decided the best way to make their attack was from above. That way, the guns would have their full maximum range of seven thousand yards, or about two and a half miles. The Germans had the same thought and fought for altitude. The battle would be fought nearly a mile and a half above London.

Henrietta was more afraid than she had ever been in her life. She began to recite to herself the words of Rudyard Kipling, who wrote:

> If you can keep your head when all about you
> Are losing theirs and blaming it on you,
> If you can trust yourself when all men doubt you,
> But make allowance for their doubting too;
> If you can wait and not be tired by waiting,
> Or being lied about, don't deal in lies,
> Or being hated, don't give way to hating,
> And yet don't look too good, nor talk too wise:

Again composed, she ordered, "Props, ahead full. Flight, up bubble ten degrees; take us to seven thousand actual."

"Ahead full, aye."

"Up bubble ten to seven thousand, aye."

"Flight, give us our altitude by thousands to six and then by hundreds."

"By thousands to six then by hundreds, aye," recently promoted flight lieutenant Pierce answered. With Lieutenant Commander Wilkinson serving as first officer, the man now in charge of tracking the enemy was Naval Lieutenant James Allen Truscott. He was next senior man to Reginald Wilkinson. Henrietta had spotted him instantly. He was clearly smart and had a good head on his shoulders. More importantly, he was one of those men whom other men followed gladly. She needed men like him to help her. She had promoted him to act as gunnery officer. He answered to "Guns."

"Guns, what is our range and bearing to target?"

"Range fifty thousand yards, bearing three two zero relative."

"Navigation, I want to split first wave. Pass the first German on the port. That will put us in the middle of them. Call the turn."

"Call the turn, first German to port, aye." After a pause, Navigation called, "Helm, port to bearing zero nine five true."

"Navigation, port to zero nine five true, aye"

The *Lady Cimarron* and the Germans were closing at better than 120 miles per hour. At that speed, battle was less than fifteen minutes away. The clock ticked down. As they got closer, Guns called the time to intercept. When at last Mr. Truscott said, "One minute to intercept," Henrietta's mind flashed to the end of Kipling's poem:

> If you can talk with crowds and keep your virtue,
> Or walk with Kings—nor lose the common touch,
> If neither foes nor loving friends can hurt you,
> If all men count with you, but none too much;
> If you can fill the unforgiving minute
> With sixty seconds' worth of distance run,
> Yours is the Earth and everything that's in it,
> And—which is more—you'll be a Man, my son.

She then added silently, *I mean a woman, my girl.*

Henrietta was stirred from her thoughts by her first officer. "Captain, some of the Germans appear to have mounted gun platforms on the tops of their ships."

"What kind of guns?"

"Light ones; they look like heavy machine guns."

"Very good. That gives them what range?"

"Theoretically, about seven thousand yards. Accurate range is closer to a third of that."

"How effective will their fire be?"

"I don't think it will amount to much. Reports from the fighting in France are that they likely use a phosphorus-based incendiary bullet. When the bullet is fired, the charge ignites and leaves a trail of blue smoke. They try for the gas bags to set us on fire."

"That won't work. This ship won't burn."

"We know that, but the Germans don't believe we're fireproof, at least according to reports in their papers."

"Even so, the spent bullets could still kill someone. Once they start burning, the others will scatter. I want them close to the point they won't be able to escape us once we engage. Mr. Wilkinson, we will commence fire at three thousand yards."

"Three thousand yards, aye. Guns, target the lead ship of each wave, then work down the lines. Stand by to commence firing."

"The leader, then down the line, aye."

Henrietta ordered, "Guns, call our range by hundreds."

"By hundreds, aye. Thirty-nine hundred and closing."

At the speed the ships were closing, Lieutenant Truscott's countdown was slow, at one and a half second intervals: "Thirty-eight..."

Mr. Wilkinson ordered, "Stand by guns."

"Thirty-seven...thirty-six." The ship flew on, and the distance closed. "Thirty-five...thirty-four...thirty-three." Henrietta took a deep breath. She could hear the fear in Mr. Truscott's voice as it rose. "Thirty-two...thirty-one...thirty..."

It was far too late to be fearful. The time for judgment was at hand. Tightening her death grip on the armrest to keep her voice steady, Henrietta said calmly, "Commence fire. Fire at will."

"Commencing fire..." The rest of the answer was lost in the thunder of the guns.

The guns stationed on the platform built out of the holds had been given detailed instructions. The forward two guns were to target the two closest ships and the aft two guns the next two out. All four of the guns fired the specially made incendiary rounds they'd been given. The aim at that range was deadly accurate, and the four German ships burst into flames. The well-practiced gun crews could fire every three seconds.

The Germans fired back ineffectively. Their rounds simply passed through the airship and fell to the ground. Had the HMA *Lady Cimarron* been filled with hydrogen, she would have been doomed. As the Germans realized what was happening, they began firing wildly. Many of the rounds fell harmlessly to the ground, but a few started fires. An alarm went off at Flight. A lucky shot from one of the doomed German airships had damaged a gas release valve. The resulting sudden increase in gas pressure threatened to overinflate the bags and bring the ship down. Sebastian ran to the site and, holding his breath, managed to close the jammed valve. He saved the ship.

One stray round crashed through the bridge, missing Henrietta by inches. The window behind her blew out with a crash. She was so terrified, she froze but didn't flinch. When she could breathe again, it was over. In just seconds, all seven of the first wave of German ships were ablaze.

The *Lady Cimarron* drove forward. The second wave was already in range and suffered the same fiery fate as the leading group. Henrietta saw the Germans were turning and trying to run with the wind. "Helm, stay after them."

"After them, aye!"

The battle turned from a slugfest into a race for life and a massacre. In minutes, the third wave was hit, burned, and was gone. The Germans in the fourth and fifth waves realized too late what they were facing. It was unlike any nightmare any had ever imagined. The surviving German airships turned away, but none was quick enough to escape. When one lone ship broke from the others, Henrietta ordered, "Let him go for now. We'll catch him after we burn the others."

In less than fifteen minutes, all that was left of the German show of force was a single ship. All of the others were now burnt-out wreckage on the ground. Henrietta turned and gave chase. It took ten long minutes to get the final German ship in range. When at last it was, a single shot hit the tail section, and the craft burst into flame.

Henrietta had remained outwardly calm during the destruction of an entire enemy fleet. The spectacle was both horrific and fascinating. When the last of the German ships, fully ablaze, started to fall, Henrietta released her grip slightly and heard her voice as though it were someone else speaking. Her words were still, soft, and calm. "Mr. Wilkinson, perhaps we should fly our large flag so those below will have no doubt as to who we are?"

Mr. Wilkinson smiled broadly. "Indeed we should, my lady." Turning to Lieutenant Truscott, he said, "Mr. Truscott, as the battle is ended, perhaps you could let the crew know?"

"Yes sir. Glad to, sir, and thank you!"

As Truscott ran back into the ship, Henrietta said, "Mr. Wilkinson, give the order."

He smiled. "Thank you, my lady. Helm, let's give those who are below something to look at. Take us in a few passes over the city. Props, ahead slow. Flight, take us down to six hundred relative and high enough to keep us from hitting anything."

HMA *Lady Cimarron* began a slow, stately descent and victory flight over London. From a hatch astern of the aft engine compartment, a thirty-by-sixty-foot flag appeared. Held by a special rigging, it rippled beneath the great ship. With the engines idling, the sound of church bells, steam whistles, and cheers could be heard aboard.

Chapter Nine:
All Hail the Hero

Flying above London, Henrietta and Mr. Wilkinson planned the trip back to Ruxmour. It would be dark by the time they got there. A night landing would be tricky with an inexperienced crew. They decided it would be safer if they took a circuitous route home. They could use the extra hours to get a little training done. They sent a wireless message to the Admiralty advising it of their plans. The reply was both a message of thanks and a request that they fly over the fleet at Rosyth. They agreed to do so the next afternoon at four.

Over the next twenty-four hours, every new crewman took his turn at every station. By completing the flight, all had earned their wings. The training was not limited to regular Royal Navy personnel. The previously civilian crew had much to learn about naval customs and traditions. By the end, everyone was exhausted.

HMA *Lady Cimarron* approached Rosyth from the west. She slowed and showed the colors. In a departure from tradition, the deck of every ship was packed with sailors anxious to see their savior. It was a spectacle worth beholding. They flew on to Edinburgh. There, the adulation they received matched in enthusiasm the response they had received when over London. After an hour, Henrietta gave the order: "Navigation, set course for Ruxmour and home. Props, ahead full. Flight, keep us at one thousand relative."

Everyone knew the new First Sea Lord John Fisher was a great believer in innovation. He greeted the idea of airships with the speed to run down a foe and kill any lesser enemy as a natural progression of technological revolution that had begun with the steam engine. The addition of women to the crew, much less having a woman as captain, was a different matter altogether. He was quite certain nothing good could come from it. Still, he could not argue with success. It appeared Henrietta had proven him wrong. He nevertheless resisted having her formally added to the list of captains in the Royal Navy. After all, she'd never served even a minute abroad a real ship. This was not a totally unreasonable position, and Lord Palmer, the political animal, knew it was time once again to compromise.

Ever since he had agreed she could serve as captain, what to do with Henrietta had been a real problem. Now that she was a national hero, it was much more than that. Lord Palmer consulted the Prime minister, and the PM consulted the king. They had an idea what to do but needed the Navy's support to implement it. The proposed solution was to have the Royal Navy form a subordinate branch, akin to the Royal Marines, to deal with Cimarrons. It would specialize in the highly unique requirements of air operations. The king had even agreed to the suggestion that it have its own ranks and allow a limited number of women to serve. Fisher and the other admirals were told of the idea but questioned the wisdom of letting women serve.

It was late afternoon by the time the *Lady Cimarron* arrived home. Attaching to the mooring mast, the ship was taken in hand by the ground crew. Only when the ship was safely in the hangar did Henrietta surrender the bridge. With the help of Lieutenant Commander Wilkinson and all of the other regular navy men, Captain Henrietta Whitfield's departure from her ship strictly complied with naval tradition. But for the fact she was a woman, she went down the gangway and ashore as would any triumphant captain of the Royal Navy.

At the base of the gangway, she was greeted by her uncle Robert, the First Lord of the Admiralty, the First Sea Lord, and a host of politicians and naval personnel. After an exchange of salutes, Lord Palmer was the first to speak. "Captain Whitfield, on behalf of His Majesty's government and a grateful nation, I must compliment you on a magnificent job. Well done."

"Thank you."

What followed was what one would expect. There were cheers and well wishes from all. Admiral Fisher for his part wanted to know the real story before he jumped into the middle of the celebration. Lieutenant Commander Wilkinson had previously served on the admiral's staff. A lieutenant assisting the admirals drew Wilkinson aside to quietly speak with the First Lord of the Admiralty and the First Sea Lord.

Admiral Fisher began, "Tell me, Mr. Wilkinson, what really happened aboard the *Lady Cimarron*? Was it you who was really in command?"

"No sir! Captain Whitfield was in charge."

"Really? She is a woman, little more than a girl."

"No sir! She is a captain and a brave one, calm and professional as any man. She never even raised her voice. I am proud to say she is my captain, and it was my honor to serve with her. I would be happy to serve with her again whenever given the opportunity."

Lord Palmer was amused, but the admiral was still not certain and shook his head.

When Lieutenant Commander Wilkinson left the room, the two men talked. Lord Palmer began, "You know this is going to start a civil war in this country over women's roles. It's bad enough right now with all of the suffragettes clamoring for the vote, but with all this....Now with a woman as the greatest national hero since Nelson, can you imagine…?"

Admiral Fisher returned, "Some won't believe it is true."

Palmer shook his head. "It won't matter. Everyone in London already does believe it."

The admiral tried again. "Some will be opposed."

"It won't matter what others might say! It is what they will say!"

The admiral gave up and frowned. He had taken the time to check Henrietta's application to the Royal Navy and had to agree that on paper she looked qualified, at least for a commission as a junior officer. He knew when it came out she had been rejected it would only add to the problem. It looked more and more like the world had flipped upside down.

Lord Palmer considered the situation. "Admiral, I for one would have challenged any man who said a woman could have done the job she did…but by God, she did it. Now who can rightly say she isn't deserving of the rank of captain and our respect?"

The First Sea Lord knew it was true. "I agree, but let's talk about this idea of a special service. I venture it may be our only way out."

Lord Palmer nodded, and Admiral Fisher continued to frown. Palmer finally spoke. "The people pushing women's suffrage are going to demand the Navy allow women serve aboard ships—"

The admiral finished the thought. “Unless we do something unthinkable.”

They rejoined the celebration, and one by one, the politicians and the admirals were consulted. At last Sebastian Cooke had his chance to speak to them. “Gentlemen, we received a wireless last night. I had the opportunity to discuss the possibility of a new service with Captain Whitfield and the others aboard.”

“How so?”

Lord Palmer said, “I wanted them to think about what I was going to propose.”

The Admiral shook his head in resignation. “Splendid. So what happened?”

“Well, the lady’s uncle, Mr. Turnbull, made plans for a new commercial Cimarron. He has gone to the trouble to design unique uniforms, badges, and ranks for everyone, including the ground crew.”

“That is interesting, but—”

“Captain Whitfield knows she’s not a sailor, but she does know about flying. When she and the others heard the suggestion that Royal Navy might establish a secondary service like the Marines for those who fly, we all agreed we’d be proud to serve in it.” Palmer said, “You know, Admiral, if the Navy goes along, we might be able to do this without throwing hundreds of years of tradition on its head.”

Sebastian added, “We were thinking if we’re not in Navy uniforms and we’re part of something different…”

Admiral Fisher finally smiled. “Lord Palmer, I know when to surrender to the inevitable. Let us go ahead with your proposed solution. After all, it can’t make the situation much worse than we find it now.”

Lord Palmer smiled. “It is not going to be easy or without controversy. Let us hope if we open its ranks to women, they can all live up to Lady Henrietta’s standards.”

With the issue of Henrietta’s role in the battle settled and the idea of a new service established, Lord Palmer and Admiral Fisher rejoined the party. They took the senior politicians and admirals aside one by one to deliver the news. Many of the politicians were appalled by the idea of recognizing Henrietta as a real captain. Their distress didn’t end there. There was open hostility by some to the idea of a new branch of service. Their anguish grew when they learned women were going to be employed as warriors. As Lord Palmer put it, “If we don’t find a way to keep Lady Henrietta in the war, the government will fall, and the next government will. More to the point, if we don't find a way, we will, as the Americans say, be lynched."

Admiral Fisher had no better time of it with the admirals. He would tell them, "If we try and force the lady out of the war, we'll find ourselves beached. If that happens, you can expect to find women aboard every ship, and who knows how many of them will be captain?"

Both men would end with a warning. "Something is happening. There is no way to stop it. We can either find a way to salvage what we can, or we can go down."

Most didn't like it, but all agreed they had to do something. Each was given a challenge. "If it is not to be a new service with a few women serving in it, then what is it to be?" No one had an answer.

After speaking to the others, Admiral Fisher and Lord Palmer had an opportunity to spend time with Henrietta. Admiral Fisher began, "Tell me, Lady Henrietta, or should I call you captain?"

Henrietta blurted out, "Oh, please, don't you start calling me that. I don't feel like a captain. I am just a woman who was thrust into the middle of the conflict. It was frightening."

The admiral was taken aback by her response. "I thought from the reports that you would be...well, I'm not certain what I thought you would be."

Lord Palmer came to the rescue. "Then, Lady Henrietta, I believe the admiral was about to ask what your plans for the future were, but now I think it is we who will tell you."

"Tell me what?"

"We—meaning the Prime minister—have consulted with the king. We have his blessing to establish a new subordinate branch of the Royal Navy. I can't tell you because no one can remember who suggested it, but the name of the new service will be called the Royal Air Service. We've decided the uniforms, ranks, and practices your uncle Robert Turnbull suggested for his airline will serve for now as those of the service."

"How exciting!"

"Lady Henrietta, more than that, women will be allowed to serve, starting with you," Lord Palmer said.

"Yes, Lady Henrietta, like it or not, you are part of this now," added the admiral. "The king and the rest of us are counting on you."

"I must tell you that I never considered..."

With a laugh, Palmer said, "A bit late for that."

"Oh dear!"

Henrietta was well and truly stuck. By morning, the government's political machine in the House of Commons was gathering steam.

Britain basked in the warmth of the *Lady Cimarron*'s victory, but the mood in Berlin was somber. The kaiser's army, having conquered Belgium and France, had been undone. It stung all the worse because the papers in Berlin had originally described Henrietta as "a girl in a balloon." Now many of his beautiful Zeppelin airships were gone, and there was nothing to show for the sacrifice.

Admiral Tirpitz was in a particularly bad mood. The admiral was famously unimpressed by the military potential of the submersible, or so-called submarine. Tirpitz embraced the American Alfred Thayer Mahon's thinking that the nation that ruled the sea also ruled the world. To do this, he advocated the Imperial German Navy build a force of large and powerful warships capable of engaging the Royal Navy. He dreamed of a battle of annihilation in the waters of the North Sea. He, just as his idol Mahan did, rejected the concept of *guerre-de-course* (or "commerce raiding") as a wasteful distraction.

While many within the German Navy considered Mahon's thinking sound, it seemed particularly short-sighted to the head of the German Army's General Staff, Field Marshal Alfred von Schlieffen. He was a self-confessed disciple of the theories of no less of an authority on war than General Carl von Clausewitz. Among the other lessons of war that he taught was that war does not consist of a single instantaneous blow. Rather, it is a series of events, the end goal of which must be to disarm the enemy. Just destroying a fleet without making it impossible for the enemy to build a new fleet only guarantees a new round of warfare in the future.

Von Schlieffen found an unlikely ally in his struggle against Tirpitz in Admiral Henning von Holtzendorf, who believed if the British were faced with a commercial blockade enforced by submarines, he could break them in as little as six months. The kaiser was intrigued by anything that he might be able to use to break the back of the Royal Navy. He knew the Royal Navy, the French Navy, and the US Navy were all building submarines. He had to keep up, so he turned to the ever-reliable engineers at Krupp. They would design and build submarines for the Imperial German Navy.

The Krupp engineers borrowed ideas liberally from designers in the United States, the United Kingdom, France, and Spain. The underwater vessels that resulted were no less amazing than Count Zeppelin's airships. Just over 220 feet long, each weighed in at an impressive 900 tons. Capable of a speed of 18 knots on the surface and 9 knots submerged, they had an impressive range of 11,000 nautical miles. They rode low in the water and possessed a periscope, and their twelve to fifteen torpedoes and two deck guns made them myopic brutes.

Tirpitz opposed building submarines but was overruled. The first submersible, or undersea boat, U-1 was built and commissioned. Tests proved so promising, the kaiser demanded a flotilla of ten such boats be constructed. Tirpitz was furious but was ultimately persuaded he could live with a limited force of submarines. They might be of some value as scouts for the fleet, as a mobile mine fleet that a superior force might be drawn into, or as raiders used to draw off British strength from the real battle. By the time the war began, Germany already had twenty-one boats, and additional boats were on order. They had been practicing in the Baltic, well away from British eyes.

The destruction of the kaiser's air armada over London was a shocking setback, but it was not the end of the war. If the Royal Navy controlled the surface of the water and the air was lost to the *Lady Cimarron*, there were still the depths of the ocean available for mischief. The disaster off Ramsgate had been made all the worse because a flotilla of eight German submarines had been present.

They were dispatched to sink ships in the Thames estuary beginning on the day following the battle. The Royal Navy ships, trying to avoid destruction from the air, ran right into them, and several ships were torpedoed and sunk. This good news for the kaiser had nearly been lost in his agony over the loss of the air armada.

Admiral Tirpitz realized if he could find a way to continue the fight against the Royal Navy, it would lift his emperor's spirit. He reported on the success of the submarines. Over dinner, the future of the war took a dark turn. If the British had a weakness, it was the fact that Britain needed trade with her empire to survive. If trade could be strangled, the lion might yet be brought to its knees. Even Tirpitz had to admit his battle fleet was no match for the British. Still, the Navy could win the war, so he called on his old political adversary Admiral Holtzendorf. He was asked to bring down Britain. Holtzendorf knew twenty-one boats were insufficient to the task. But he also knew by the end of the evening that every shipyard in Germany capable of building undersea boats would be receiving contracts within days. It would not take long for the new machines to find their way to him.

An uneasy calm settled over Europe. The German army made itself at home in France. This time, the kaiser would disarm France once and for all. Count Zeppelin went back to the drawing board. Now that the value of helium was clear, the Germans needed a source of it for themselves. A recovery facility was built near Odolanów in Prussia, but its production was limited. A second plant was built in French Algeria near the town of Arzew. The count assured the kaiser that the next time the airships met in battle, it would be the Germans who prevailed. While the Germans' attempt to keep their discovery of helium secret, word got out, and the British were aware of what was coming.

In Britain, it was still politics as usual. The very unpopular Conservative government resigned, and Sir Henry Campbell-Bannerman became Prime minister. Baron Tweedmouth took over as First Lord of the Admiralty, and Lloyd George became the president of the Board of Trade. It was a calculated risk. The Conservatives assumed the Liberals would make a mess of the war and end up losing in a landslide at the next election. As the war dragged on, the cost of preparations continued to mount. The Liberals were forced to hold firm on taxes and tariffs to pay for the expenses and were unable to fulfill promises regarding public education and health care. As prices for staples creeped up, the electorate started to become disenchanted, and it looked as if the political gamble might pay off for the Conservatives.

A mind-numbing cacophony from the politicians began deafening everyone. As they wrangled for control of Parliament, it seemed the war itself was unimportant. Despite this, the excitement surrounding Lady Henrietta continued unabated. Henrietta was amazed. She was just a girl who had gotten a little carried away when duty called. She told Uncle Robert, "I am not a soldier. What am I going to do?"

"Like it or not, you are a soldier in the king's service. You have to do your duty and see this war through to the end."

"To the end?"

"Dear, the war is still on. The whole country, the whole world thinks of you as the warrior queen who saved Britain."

"But I was scared to death."

"Of course it was scary, but it is who you are now. Others are counting on you, and, as I say, you're going to have to see it through."

"But—"

"No buts. You're the one who said she could do it. Now that they believe you, you can't let them down."

Henrietta thought about it. Fate had taken a hand in her life, and now it was well beyond her control.

The press trumpeted Henrietta's achievement, likening it to the defeat of the Spanish Armada and the rout of Napoleon at Waterloo. They began a drumbeat on her behalf, arguing that if ever someone was owed a debt for extraordinary service to the Crown, she was Henrietta. The king was amused.

To say the king and his nephew, Kaiser Wilhelm of Germany, did not get along was an understatement. The king, for his part, found "little Willie" a bit arrogant and somewhat obnoxious. The kaiser was proud of being emperor of Germany and possessor of all of its supposed military prowess. After his army's victory over France, he claimed with Field Marshall von Schlieffen and his General Staff in charge that Germany could overrun England in a fortnight. The kaiser called his uncle Bertie "the old peacock." Matters were made worse by the fact that the Danish-born Queen Alexandra loathed Wilhelm, never forgetting that the Prussians had seized Schleswig-Holstein from Denmark in the 1860s. She poisoned the relationship of the two men.

Now a woman who was little more than a girl had very publicly undone the kaiser and all of his generals. It left the kaiser the laughingstock of Europe. Many accused him of having failed to read his history lessons. What kind of a silly fool tries sending an armada against Britain?

When the Prime minister suggested Henrietta be given a rank and title of her own, the king did him one better. He invited Henrietta and her mother to Buckingham Palace for a private tea. The king took an instant liking to the attractive, young, and intelligent lady-tomboy. By the end of the afternoon, he had invited her to return, and she'd offered to take him aloft whenever he'd like. The king told her how grateful he was that she had put that arrogant little popinjay Wilhelm back on his heels. Then with a smile, he took a swipe at the

German General Staff by naming her the Air Marshall of Britain. Then he named her a Duchess of Azure, taking the name Azure from the old Anglo-French word for the color of the light and unclouded sky, the sky that nearly all in Britain proclaimed she was the queen of.

The king had not been kidding. The Duchy of Azure was created by letters patent. The duchy included a special remainder that allowed it to pass to the daughters of the first duchess in default of a son, and then to the heirs of those daughters, be they granddaughters or grandsons. When Henrietta brought HMA *Lady Cimarron* down to London just to take the king on a brief flight, he presented her with her sky-blue field marshal's baton. Her mother, Beatrice, was beyond ecstatic. Her little girl had managed to crack the highest ranks of British society, and she wasn't even married yet.

Chapter Ten:
A Lady's Grace

With the ownership of the Cimarron Airship Company, Her Grace, the Duchess of Azure was not just beautiful but also fabulously wealthy and a national hero. What had been a flood of invitations and proposals of marriage became a deluge.

Henrietta now owned Ruxmour Manor. The social demands on the household were overwhelming the staff. One of the young maids was so exhausted at the end of one day, she passed out in the hallway just outside Henrietta's room. Henrietta helped get her to bed and discovered the wretched conditions the staff was enduring. She'd known they were crowded, but this was ridiculous. When she looked at the books, she discovered how little the staff was paid. It was entirely unacceptable for people to work in her house, live in a tenement like a pack of rats, and work themselves to death for slave wages.

The next morning, Henrietta announced to all her staff their situation was to change now that she was in charge. She said, "I know that this is Britain and there are rules, but I spent my early life in America where things are different. The class distinctions that separate people here do not exist there. That is why I am going to think of this house as just like a ship. You and I serve together aboard her. I do not consider you my servants; we are crewmates. As my crewmates, I intend to get to know each of you and treat you with the respect you should have.

"Now, I'd like to begin by inviting Mr. Danvers, the butler, to come and have tea with me in the library at ten this morning. Tomorrow I will ask Mrs.

MacGregor, the housekeeper, to join me. After that, as my schedule permits, I am going to sit down with each of you so I get to know you individually."

Henrietta immediately commandeered the workers who were building another new barracks for flight crews and had them complete the work on the servants' quarters, giving everyone a room of his or her own. She also raised everyone's salary. The biggest change was she hired additional staff so that the workday could be shortened to eight hours. Her mother was a little uncertain about the wisdom of Henrietta's generosity, asking, "Are you absolutely certain you want to toss the whole of English society into the cinder bucket?"

"Mother, don't worry. I know what I am doing. I intend to bring a little of America's promise of a better life here, that's all." Very quickly, Henrietta found herself surrounded by a grateful and loyal staff.

Henrietta was speaking earnestly when she said she would get to know the staff individually. She had tea with each privately. She told each one, "I may be Your Grace, but I want you to be my friend. As friends, I expect we will acknowledge each other with at least a smile when we meet in the hall. I also expect my friends to speak honestly to me and tell me what they think and what I need to be told. I do not just want to be told what I want to hear."

She referred to them collectively as the Ruxmour crew. The first time she showed up in the kitchen, she told the cook, Mrs. Wiggins, "This is your kitchen. I'm just here to take my turn on kitchen duty. I am a good cook, and I'd like to help, but put me to work as you see fit. I'll wash dishes if that is all you can find for me to do."

"But why, Your Grace, why? Why would you want to do that?"

"It is nothing I haven't done before, and it is nothing I am too proud to do now. Anyway, I find it hard to ask others to do things I can't or won't do myself."

Now that Henrietta and her mother lived in a more normal environment, Beatrice softened and actually was very nice to be around. She didn't cook very well but did help the maids tidy up every now and again.

Within weeks, the house was a cheery place to work. Gone were the sad, tired faces that turned away when Henrietta walked down the hall. They were replaced by smiles. Even the dowdy maid's uniforms were gone. The female crew members wore tailored and properly fitted black outfits with white collars and turnback white cuffs, or more frequently, a skirt with a high-collar blouse favored by Henrietta herself. In the house, the maid's caps were dispensed with. The staff was free to wear their hair up in the style that best suited them and to use ribbons, bows, or headbands to keep hair out of their eyes. Henrietta did provide a military-style coat and cap to be worn when out of doors. The cap was a variation on Margaretha's attempt at a military bonnet. Instead of the company badge, Henrietta had a jeweler make up a brooch and matching lapel pin in the form of the Celtic dragon on her crest. The girls loved the new outfits. However, the favorite new item of clothing was rubber gloves with a cotton flocking on the inside. These protected the girls' hands when cleaning. With a virtually unlimited supply of starched fitted aprons to be worn only when actually cooking or cleaning, the girls looked more like daughters of the house than servants. The uniforms were so nice, the girls asked and were given permission to wear them when out of the house.

The no fraternization policy among aircrews had the unintended consequence of leaving the girls serving at Ruxmour in great demand by the young men in cadet training. In their new "Ruxmours," as the maids' dress came to be known, the girls became the envy of their peers. The outfits soon became a fashion craze. The reputation of Ruxmour was a bit quirky, but without doubt, it was the best house in all of Britain to serve in.

With the Battle of London behind it, the new Royal Air Service got down to the business of building a true air fleet. Despite some complaints in the US Congress, the export of helium to Britain began in earnest. At Ruxmour Manor, the first new Cimarron built by the Cimarron Airship Company was christened HMA *Lady Beatrice* in honor of Henrietta's mother. That established the naming practice for all "Lady-class" Cimarrons that followed. They included the *Lady Charlotte*, the *Lady Mary*, the *Lady Margaretha*, and the *Lady Jane*.

Asking Henrietta to be both the leader of the Cimarron Airship Company and the Royal Air Service was too much. Uncle Robert persuaded his friend and president of the American Airship Company, Philip Andrew, to stay on and run the business side of the company. Meanwhile, Uncle Robert decided to build a second Cimarron yard in England near his other estate named Thorndale Abby. He considered forming a new company but decided against it, instead opting to go into partnership with his niece's company. Once the new facility was in operation, Uncle Robert returned to America to deal with his other business interests. Henrietta's cousin James had been left in charge. Uncle Robert wanted to see how his new young partner was doing now that he'd fallen in love with a nice American girl and they had opted to make their home in America so she could be near her family.

Henrietta busied herself throughout, training new flight crews. When the new Royal Air Service, or RAS, announced it was seeking volunteers, thousands applied. When it was learned women were allowed to serve, thousands more applied. The new service could afford to be selective. Applicants seeking consideration for flight training had to be physically fit and of good moral character. Every applicant needed to have some college education, if not a degree, and could not be afraid of heights. Those who were willing to serve with the ground crew were required to be of good moral character and have some skill or training the service was in need of. Those already serving in the Navy, Army, or Marines could apply for a transfer, but all transfers were subject to approval of the new service. To help winnow the herd and after some serious consultation with Admiral Fisher, all applicants had to sign up for a minimum of three years or the duration of the war, whichever was longer. To rid themselves of girls shopping for a husband, they also made it clear that a strict policy against fraternization would be rigidly enforced. Still, there was no shortage of volunteers.

In the first class of cadets, one girl stood out—Lidya Milonov Ives. Lidya was very much interested in science and mathematics. While still in her late teens, she had lived in America when her father was posted there. It had rubbed off on her. She had come home to England and managed to gain admission to the University of London. She was a dark-haired beauty with dark, intelligent eyes. Very athletic for a woman, she could be alarmingly intimidating when it suited her purpose. She, like Henrietta, had decided to wait to marry until after she was educated. She was more mature than many of her classmates. It was clear from the start that she and Henrietta would get along splendidly. Upon graduation, Lydia attained the rank of flying officer. She was then assigned to act as an aide to Henrietta. Up until Lidya joined the staff, Margaretha, who had become Henrietta's best friend, had her hands full. Lidya was a perfect fit, and she helped ease the burden on both Margaretha and Flight Leader Pierce, who now served as the air marshal's aid-de-camp.

When the second ship, HMA *Lady Beatrice*, was commissioned, Henrietta offered its command to newly promoted flight commander Wilkinson, but he declined, insisting Mr. Cooke was the only one who was truly ready to take on the role. Sebastian objected, but Henrietta pointed out if she had no choice in the matter, neither did he. He became Flight Captain Sebastian Cooke and made his father so proud, there were no words.

After Henrietta was promoted to air marshal, she became in effect an admiral, and she could no longer command a ship of her own directly. This happy accident resulted in Commander Wilkinson agreeing to accept a promotion and serve as her flag captain.

Margaretha, freed from the burden of looking after Henrietta with Lidya now taking on that role, was able to move away with her husband. Because Alexander and Margaretha were Americans, they were barred from service in the war. This left them free to move to Thorndale Abby, now simply known as Thorndale, and for Alexander to become the company's vice president in charge of production. When Uncle Robert bought the property, the very distinctive neoclassical primary house was in great need of repair or replacement. He decided to retain the exterior but upgrade the interior to modern standards. The estate that surrounded the house would be the home of his primary European airship plant. The new Thorndale plant and the original facility at Ruxmour would produce the Cimarron warships the British needed. The commercial airships that Uncle Robert hoped for were to be built in America.

Uncle Robert turned the house over to Alexander and Margaretha. As at Ruxmour, the house would serve as their home and the center of a small community of fliers and others working for the company. The manufacturing plant included four hangars and several support buildings needed to construct Cimarrons. The hangars were large enough to construct airships up to nine hundred feet long. It was to be Alexander's responsibility as the vice president in charge of production to make it work.

Meanwhile, Henrietta, the Duchess of Azure, and her mother, Beatrice, the Dowager Countess of Hardingham, tried to make an English lady out of Margaretha. The ladies had an almost impossible task. The most difficult part was just getting Margaretha to accept the fact her staff would address her as a baroness. She was to be Lady VonKleist or my lady. Technically, her husband was a German baron, so it was expected. As she was born and raised in American, it seemed kind of silly. To make the point that the title was mandatory, Henrietta told her, "I understand using titles seems silly to Americans like us, but over here, the title comes with the house. Accept it or move back to dusty Oklahoma."

Once the matter of her title was settled, Margaretha's primary responsibility became running the house and entertaining guests. She had no idea how an English lady would go about such tasks. Henrietta and Beatrice suggested she use the approach pioneered at Ruxmour. With the help of several members of the Ruxmour staff who were willing to relocate, Margaretha settled in. Her "Americanized" English country house featured a smiling and happy staff in smart new uniforms. Alexander would swell with pride when he spoke of his lady and her efforts.

The new ships to be built at Thorndale were 800 feet long and 135 feet in diameter. Powerful new engines gave them a top speed of 135 kilometers per hour, or better than 85 miles an hour. After the battle, the designers had gone to work. They had the advantage of having seen the battle damage to the *Lady Cimarron*. From it, they concluded rightly that shooting holes in the gas bags was virtually useless. Hits to components such as engines and gas-handling equipment were the key to stopping an airship. Tests revealed that using a low rate of cannon fire and high-explosive ordinance was less likely to achieve significant damage than were lesser shots from a rapid-fire gun that could redirect its fire quickly.

Calling on American designers, they developed a very heavy machine gun firing an impressive two-pounder or 40 mm shell at a rate of more than 120 per minute. The new ships would be armed primarily with these weapons, but a pair of six-pounders would also be carried for surface bombardment. The British tried to use a heavier gun but a slow rate of fire and the weight of the recoil system to prevent damage to the ship made it unacceptable. Lastly, the ships would retain bomb-carrying capacity but in only one hold and not the two of the Lady class.

Only four months after construction began, the first new ship, the HMA *Queen Elizabeth*, took flight. Her sister, the *Queen Victoria*, was launched a month later, and they were followed by the *Queen Anne* and *Queen Caroline* at six-week intervals. Even with massive amounts of overtime and extra staff, Thorndale would be pressed to produce more than six ships the first year. The Lady-class ships were also to remain in production. They were a proven design and far cheaper and quicker to produce. They would be built at Ruxmour.

Lady-class ships were being launched every four weeks, and by year's end, there would be eleven of them including the *Lady Cimarron*. Armed with the new lighter guns and a single six-pounder, they remained formidable.

The *Queen Elizabeth* was a wonderful ship. She was more powerful than her sisters of the Lady class and roomy enough to accommodate a battle staff. Henrietta decided it would serve as the flagship of the new RAS fleet.

Before she relocated, she went to Buckingham Palace again to have tea with the king. He had taken a liking to his spunky young lady warrior. The setting was informal now that she was a peer, and she felt bold enough to speak her mind if something needed to be said. "As Your Majesty is aware, I am to date the only flag officer of the Royal Air Service despite its growth. Even so, I have detected a little resistance to the idea of appointing someone as my deputy."

"So you have someone in mind?"

"I do. He is my flag captain, Reginald Wilkinson. As you know, he is the most senior of all of our Royal Navy transfers to the RAS. He has been with me since the beginning and should be recognized as my deputy."

"Deputy?"

"Promoted to air vice marshal."

"I see. What do the admirals think?"

"Well, I know that he worked for Admiral Fisher and that he considers him more than competent."

"Then in that case, you have my blessing, but please do keep peace with Jackie and the rest of the Navy. Ask him rather than tell him."

The idea of promoting a senior and experienced naval officer appealed to the Admiralty, many of whom feared the new service would be taken over by women. With the admirals' blessings, Captain Wilkinson became Air Vice Marshal Wilkinson. He, to use the naval term, hoisted his pennant on the *Queen Victoria* only days after she was declared operational. The *Queen Elizabeth* would need a new captain. Henrietta considered offering the job to Sebastian, but he was happy where he was, so she offered the job to James Truscott. He'd proven himself at the Battle of London and had since command the *Lady Jane*. He was honored and accepted the job eagerly.

Wilkinson and Truscott were not the only men who had served with Henrietta during the Battle of London. Sebastian had been careful in whom he picked from the volunteers, and all had the makings of extraordinary officers. Nearly all now served as captains or first officers aboard the new ships of the RAS. They trusted their air marshal, and she trusted them. Their crews all went through training at Ruxmour and aboard the venerable *Lady Cimarron* herself. Even so, each captain made certain every member of their own crews knew Henrietta's story and of their personal bond to her.

In addition to training and comradeship, British crews also enjoyed the advantage of a new invention in the form of a folded parachute that could be worn in a soft backpack. Ever since the Battle of London, it had bothered many that all of the Germans died because none had a safe way to abandon their stricken ships. Now that the Germans were using helium, any future battle would likely be far more difficult to win, and British airships might be lost. Credit for the device went to a Major David Somerset-Moss, who considered the problem one evening at dinner. A waiter unfolded a napkin with a flourish and waved it like a flag before placing it in another diner's lap. The major was inspired. "What if a parachute could be folded in such a way that it would open on its own?" The folded parachute gave a falling man a chance to survive. The major and his friends thought more aggressively. If one could minimize the risk of falling to one's death, perhaps one might consider boarding an enemy vessel in flight. There were other ideas put forward. As crazy as some of them sounded, volunteers began trying to figure out ways to accomplish the impossible.

The men who would try such a thing were a breed apart. They were part of the RAS, but just like the Royal Marines, they were going to take on the role of light infantry. They were volunteers drawn from the Army as well as the Marines. After a lively discussion as to what they were to be called, Henrietta settled the squabble by calling them her special airship soldiers, or the SAS for short. The uniform all would wear was the next bone of contention. Because what they were planning to do involved jumping, it didn't take the horsemen long to suggest jodhpur-inspired polo outfits. A special harness was worn over their military jackets. The men discovered that the parachute lines could entangle them on landing, so each harness came equipped with a razor-sharp "jump knife." Worn with black riding boots, the look proved particularly practical to jump in. Several of Henrietta's RAS companions tried the new style for themselves and thought it looked very dashing, as distinctive as shipboard flight gear. Soon jodhpurs began appearing throughout the Cimarrons.

Despite some half-hearted protests, Henrietta put women aboard every ship. The inclusion of women in the crews of the Cimarrons had not sparked nearly as much controversy as what happened when it came to parachutes. One simply cannot parachute in any type of skirt or dress. Because of this, Henrietta made the practical decision that if flight crew members, including the women, were to have parachutes, they all needed to wear some type of pants with their uniform jackets while onboard ship. Thanks to inspiration from the young soldiers and the work of several seamstresses, Henrietta had new uniforms pants in the form of modified jodhpurs made for her and several other women. They were not so unladylike as to offend.

The last addition to Henrietta's uniform was a pistol belt. Henrietta's reputation as a pistol shot had followed her from her first days at Cimarron. It, combined with her enjoyment of dime novels about cowboys and shootouts, led many young army officers to suggest she wear a holstered pistol. It would serve as a reminder that she was the new marshal in town and stood ready to take on anyone foolish enough to try. She, after all, was the foremost warrior of the twentieth century and could take care of herself. A black leather holster and belt with a silver buckle was added to everyone's uniform. RAS officers, both men and women, had an elegant but unmistakable military look about them.

Henrietta led a group of women through mandatory parachute training and leapt from the HMA *Queen Elizabeth* while five thousand feet over the Salisbury Plain. On learning of her activities, Beatrice was distressed. "Henrietta! What in the world would possess you to jump out of a perfectly good Cimarron?"

"Mother, I won't say it wasn't frightening and that I wasn't terrified, but it had to be done. I am the leader of the RAS, and I cannot ask others to do what I will not do myself. A leader must lead by example."

"I understand, but please do not get yourself killed in the process. It is not the kind of example you want others to follow."

Once the RAS established that men and women could safely jump from a Cimarron, the next logical step was to find a means to get someone back on board. With the Navy well represented, it did not take long for someone to come up with the idea of using the bomb winch and a boatswain's chair. A winch with 2,500 feet of wire rope was developed. The justification for the expense was it could be used to lift supplies or men without having to land.

The first test of the system was very promising. HMA *Lady Alice* came to a dead stop. It dropped a line and then hoisted a mailbag on board. Several more loads were pulled up without difficulty. Flying Officer Tommy Fawkes gained the distinction of being the first man to try the system. It worked just as hoped. Further tests showed that if the *Lady Alice* was still under way, she didn't need to stop if flying slowly. The line needed to be only long enough to grab and attach to before the ship lifted up. If a man was fitted with a parachute jumping harness, the shock was no greater than when parachuting.

Henrietta was willing to fling herself into the air to prove a point. It only added to her mystique when she insisted she be hoisted aboard the *Lady Alice* to prove it could be done safely. It took a brave man to do the things she did. Many considered it foolhardy, but it was a carefully thought-out effort on her part to remain one of "the few." Although many older women found the thought of wearing pants unsettling, younger women embraced the new look, and soon women in jodhpurs on the streets of London became a common sight. After all, the pants weren't dissimilar to the bicycle outfits that were becoming popular. Worn with high-heel riding boots, the girls looked very jaunty.

The members of the SAS were not content to limit their innovations to uniforms and parachutes. They wanted special weapons as well. The logical place to begin was the machine gun. It proved its worth as early as 1893 during the First Matabele War in Rhodesia, when a machine gun designed by Hiram Maxim profoundly changed the nature of war. During the Battle of the Shangani, 700 soldiers fought off 5,000 warriors with just four Maxim guns. This success was repeated during the German conquest of France. The only problem was that machine guns were heavy and awkward to move about.

On a visit to Britain, Uncle Robert spoke with some of the men who were experimenting with boarding an airship in air. They told him what they needed was a much lighter and more mobile gun so a single man might carry it. In the tight confines of an airship, long-range and powerful rifle cartridges were unnecessary; better, they suggested, a weapon that fired a pistol-caliber bullet. Uncle Robert listened. Always willing to embrace new ideas, he went to John Browning and the Colt's Patent Firearms Manufacturing Company and commissioned prototypes of very light machine guns to fire pistol-caliber bullets. The effort hadn't produced anything workable yet, but he held out hope someday it would.

Chapter Eleven:
The Perils of Romance

With all that was going on, Henrietta was still expected to attend a certain number of social functions. When one isn't covered with work, parties and balls can be fun. When one is covered, they are a nuisance that must be endured.

The constant attention of suitors was more than annoying. Henrietta and her mother had long since made peace, and it was nice to have at least one other person in the world who was looking out for her best interests. Henrietta asked her mother, "What am I to do? I am being drowned by men!"

"Henrietta, there is only one way to put a stop to all of it."

"What?"

"Get married."

"I don't want to get married."

"Well then, at least get engaged. Once you are spoken for, the others, if they are gentlemen, will leave you alone. Until then, you are fair game."

"Mother, I'm not a rabbit or a fox!"

"To them you are. You are a prize they all want to win."

"Oh dear, I don't want to be that."

"That is the way the world is. Do any of them like you for who you are and not whom you've become?"

"Well, there's the Marquis of Cheviot. You remember Coinneach."

"That boy you used to like when—"

"Back before his father was posted to India."

"He was very nice, as I recall."

"Yes, him. I saw him at the ball. He called me Henri."

"He what?"

"When I was just a girl, don't you remember he and Daddy would tease me?"

"And he still does?"

"Yes, sometimes. I call him Connie."

"Why on Earth...?"

"He uses a boy's name to address me; it's only fair I tease him back."

"Oh dear. So, he calls you Henry?"

"Yes, Henri, when he's not staring up into the sky."

"Why does he stare at the sky?"

"He's an astronomer. He's got an observatory north of us."

"Anything else you want to tell me about him?"

"No, I think that's most of it."

"Is he interested in you? I mean, would he be interested in courting you?"

"They all are. That's the problem."

"Do you like him?"

"Of course. Connie has always been fun to be around. He even kissed me at the duke's party."

"Then I have a suggestion."

"What?"

"Tell him your problem. Ask him if he has any idea how to fix it."

"Mother, that's a little forward. It would be very presumptuous of me. He'll think I want him to propose."

"That wouldn't be the end of the world. He is a marquis and the heir to his father's title, and, well, desperate times require desperate solutions."

"Mother!"

Beatrice decided to exercise her mother's prerogative. The time had come to matchmake and meddle. She invited the Lord Cheviot to dinner. Right after the ball Henrietta had tried to put Connie out of her mind by telling herself he was just a man and not the imaginary Prince Charming she'd built up in her mind. Now that she had seen him grown up some of the fun she'd had imagining what he might be like was gone. Still, she wasn't too disappointed. For a man he'd turned out to be more than satisfactory. But satisfactory or not, when she found out what her mother had done, she was annoyed.

"Mother, how could you?" complained Henrietta.

"I could because I am your mother, and Mother knows best."

"Mother!"

Dinner turned out to be pleasant after all. Connie, the man, was in fact very charming. He didn't give a hoot about flying and was interested only in the RAS because Henrietta was involved with it. It was refreshing to not be pestered with flattery and proposals. Connie invited Henrietta to come down and look at the stars with him. Had anyone else asked, she'd have said no. It would have been only an excuse to get her alone in the moonlight. With Connie, she'd actually get to look at the stars. They agreed that the next clear night, she would join him.

The Duchess of Azure dragged Flying Officer Lidya along on the adventure. Her aide's reward was the company of a charming assistant to Lord Cheviot by the name of Peter Moore. It was a moonless, clear night, and the four of them watched until dawn.

"Henrietta, I think the universe is much larger than anyone suspects," said Connie.

"How big?"

"Some of us think that the nebulae are other galaxies. Who knows how many there are? But I'm guessing hundreds or even thousands."

"That's hard to imagine," Henrietta said in amazement

"Not everyone agrees with me. I am trying to find the proof I need to show I'm right." Connie went on to explain how he was going to do it. It sounded laborious and boring, but his eyes lit up as he spoke, and Henrietta felt herself being drawn in. She rather enjoyed being in the moonlight with him. It was refreshing to spend time with someone who wanted to talk about real stars and not just about the stars in her eyes.

On a cloudy and overcast night, a week later, Connie came to dinner. The next day, he and Henrietta went on a picnic. It was her turn to talk to him about the clouds. She'd learned to read them as a sailor reads the waves. She told him about her childhood dreams of sailing through the clouds and seeing the world from above. Aside from her trusted friend Air Vice Marshal Wilkinson (who was married and had a beautiful wife and two small children) and her Uncle Robert, Connie was one of the few men she could really talk to without being bombarded with flattery or a proposal.

Over the coming weeks, Henrietta made two more trips to the observatory, and they had tea or dined together at least once a week. Connie's latest discovery had something to do with a type of star known as a Cepheid variable. When he explained what he'd found, it made very little sense to Henrietta, but he got so excited when he spoke, she just marveled. Connie was just as lost as when Henrietta talked about flying and the RAS.

The good thing was that astronomy and flying weren't the only things they liked. They shared a wide range of other interests, which made them happy to talk for hours. They both found it terribly funny that when they had been kids, Henrietta had always been accused of having the stars in her eyes, and Connie was the down-to-earth one. Now it was the other way around, and it was delightful. Henrietta found that when she had a chance to spend time with Connie, she always returned in a remarkably good mood. Connie liked Henrietta as well. It was obvious to everyone what was developing between them. Even so, Connie maintained his distance and never spoke about their relationship. At last, Henrietta could stand it no more.

One afternoon as they stood peering out the window at the clouds building on the horizon, Henrietta was holding onto Connie's arm. It was so pleasant and comfortable. Being very relaxed around him, she felt she could talk to him about whatever was on her mind. She began, "You do know, of course, that I am very fond of you, don't you?"

"Yes. At least I've always hoped so."

"Are you fond of me?"

"Yes, absolutely."

"Then why, if I may ask, have you never mentioned that fact?"

"I thought it would annoy you."

"Annoy me? Why would you say that?"

"I know that having every man in the world after you is distressing."

"Who told you that? My mother?"

"No, I haven't spoken to her, but I do have eyes and ears."

"So you figured it out on your own."

"Yes, I did. You see, I know what it feels like to be a prize beef up for auction."

"Really?"

"Yes, really. You know, over the years, people—meaning my own mother in particular—have tried to play matchmaker. She and they have introduced me to numerous pretty young ladies."

Henrietta giggled. "So why didn't you pick one and get married? Weren't they pretty enough?"

"Oh, that wasn't it. Matter of fact, some of them looked a lot like you."

"So you don't like the way I look?"

"Oh! No, there is absolutely nothing wrong with the way you look. I think you are the prettiest girl I've ever met."

"Thank you."

"They were pretty enough…but when I'd get up close, I'd see they were basically empty shells. Everything about them was on the outside. It was like talking to a cat. You might say the lights were on, but no one was at home."

"I see. So, being pretty made them stupid?"

"No! No, it is just that…well, the most attractive thing about you is what's inside you."

"Inside me? Well, if something inside me makes me so attractive, then tell me what that is."

"It's that I've never met anyone like you. You are you! Smart and strong and, well…your own person and…the kind of woman I'd like to spend my life with."

"If you feel that way, why not tell me?"

"Because, well…OK, what would you say if I asked you to marry me?"

"Are you asking me or—?"

Connie pulled Henrietta around so she faced him, and he kissed her. Pulling back, he put his fingers on her lips. "Henrietta, I know you get carried away sometimes, like when you demanded to be captain, and…I don't want you to regret your answer. This is too important." She nodded. "Henrietta, would you make me the happiest man in the world and marry me? Don't answer me now. Think about it first; then tell me."

Before she could answer, he kissed her again. They fell silent. After that, Connie left without another word.

Henrietta thought about Connie's proposal through the night. In fact, it was all she could think about for the next several days. Connie wasn't like the other men she knew. He liked her for what she was. What would her life be if her husband were that kind of a man? She resolved she would give Connie her answer when she saw him at his father's home.

The duke held an annual winter ball, and she was expected to attend. Connie would be there too. She had attended several balls since she had been made a duchess. On nights she was willing to put up with the foolishness of young men, she would wear a gown and go dancing. On nights she wasn't in the mood, she wore her formal RAS dress uniform and refused every request. For the duke's ball, she decided a gown was required. The one she chose was a confection of white and sky-blue silk. Like all of her favorite dresses, it was made to waltz in.

When she arrived, she greeted her host. Between those of equal rank, titles were generally ignored, but Henrietta had always addressed Connie's father and mother as "Your Grace," and there seemed no need to change that.

She stood chatting with the duke and duchess as Connie made his way across the room to join them. Before he arrived, the first of Henrietta's prospective dance partners, the son of an earl, offered himself up. As Connie stepped close, she told the young man, "I'm sorry; I must decline. My dance card is full. I've reserved every dance this evening for my Lord Cheviot."

Connie, on hearing that, said softly, "Henrietta, does that mean you've made up your mind?"

She whispered back, "It does. The answer is yes. I will marry you."

"Well then, I guess I should make it official."

"How do you think you're going to do that?"

"Like this." Connie stepped passed Henrietta and whispered to his mother, "You can stop all of your scheming to marry me off. I have some good news."

"What is it?"

"I'm engaged to be married."

"To whom, my dear?"

Holding out his hand to his bride to be, he said, "Why, to the beautiful and alluring Henrietta."

His mother gasped, "Our duchess?"

"Yes, the one and only Duchess of Azure."

Connie's father, who had been listening, perked up. He had been feeling his age and his infirmity, but this was wonderful news. "Let me be the first to congratulate you both. May I make an announcement?"

Henrietta smiled. "Please do. I'm afraid my mind is made up, and your son is not going to get out of his proposal now."

With that, the older man tottered away to the orchestra leader. A moment later, there was a fanfare. Henrietta's mother had been correct when she said once Henrietta was spoken for, most of the proposals and pursuits would stop. Of course, some still held out hope, but she was decided. She and Connie danced the evening away. A date for the wedding was set for the following summer. Preparations for such an event take time, and there was a war on.

Chapter Twelve:
Politics

Leading both a new military service and an unintended fashion revolution was not all that Henrietta was asked to do. Though proposals of marriage stopped, Henrietta continued to be badgered with requests for her time, money, and influence. One such request was made by the prime minister's sister-in-law, Lady Frances Balfour. She was the president of the Central Society for Women's Suffrage. She asked Henrietta to join her effort. Henrietta declined, saying, "Lady Balfour, I am presently involved in one war. I cannot get involved in another."

"May I then list you as a supporter of our cause?"

"No, I am in service to the king. Unless he expresses his approval, I will not take a position that might go against his wishes."

"But you are the perfect example of what a woman might hope to become."

"Then use me as an example, but I cannot join your struggle." Henrietta gave much the same answer to many who sought her endorsement.

This was not to say Henrietta did not have her causes. She made sure everyone who worked for her was paid well and had at least some time off to enjoy it. She made no distinction between men and women in this regard, saying, "I pay people for the job they do, not their gender."

She also believed in education, so all those who lived near her home at Ruxmour and at the company's facilities at Thorndale, whether they worked directly for the RAS or the company or not, enjoyed the benefit of free education for their children and proper medical attention. For those who were lucky enough to work directly in the household, she brought in instructors and teachers. When asked by a reporter, "Why do you do it all?" she famously remarked, "One might be born with a title, but if one wants respect, he or she must earn it. If I am to be respected, I must do something to deserve it. I never forget I was a child of parents who had to work hard for a living before noble titles came to them. That memory is why I do what I can for those who are still working toward the future."

The Baroness VonKleist was not so constrained and became deeply involved in efforts both to obtain the vote and to improve the working conditions and pay for women everywhere. Her husband's role in the Cimarron Airship Company and her close friendship with the Duchess Azure were well known. Matched with her plainspoken directness, it made the baroness a formidable ally in any struggle.

Through the long, quiet months of winter, the war slipped into the background. Henrietta and Connie had the luxury of living near each other and spent time together frequently. As the days passed, Henrietta became more and more convinced she'd made the correct decision regarding her future.

The Germans appeared content to sit it out until spring. As spring turned to summer and nothing happened, everyone began to relax. The fall of France and the Battle of London marked the end of the first few frenetic weeks of the war. Those terrifying events were fading into memory like a bad dream. There had been some concern that fighting might erupt in Denmark, but both the Germans and the British wanted to avoid an entanglement that might bring the Danes in. Against this backdrop, both sides agreed to respect Danish neutrality. The German fleet remained in port or contented itself practicing in the Baltic, so there were no major naval engagements, although there was an ongoing cruiser war in the Pacific. Britain's trade with America was uninterrupted, and for the most part, Germany also could still trade all but war goods across the Atlantic.

On May 21st, Uncle Robert inaugurated commercial passenger service by Cimarron across the Atlantic. The Airship America Line's airship AA *Blue Horizon* made its first crossing from New York to London, landing at Osterley Manor Air Terminal. Robert had acquired the property from the Earl of Jersey as part of a larger transaction with the Earl's private bank, Childs & Co. The open area surrounding the manor house proved perfect for Cimarron operations. The *Blue Horizon* was one several ships that began offering weekly service. The other Cimarrons were the AA *Fascination*, AA *Imagination*, and AA *Ecstasy*. Robert assured the public that more ships would be added to the fleet as demand for service increased.

On the continent, peace was still elusive. The civil war in what had been the Austro-Hungary Empire had gone from bad to worse. Ethnic strife and nationalistic fervor destroyed the dual monarchy, leaving the German-speaking minority in a desperate state. An earlier Austro-Hungary revolution had begun in 1848 and had been put down with Russian and Prussian help. This time around, no such help was available. Rumored to be insane because of inbreeding by the Hapsburg family, the new emperor, Franz Ferdinand, could not hope to hold on. Large parts of his army revolted, and he ultimately fled for his life. Fearing reprisals and wholesale slaughter, elements within Austria begged the Germans to intervene. Some even went so far as to offer the crown of Austria to the kaiser. The German leader was cautious. After an incident that resulted in the deaths of several hundred Austrians, the plea was answered, and the German army intervened. The occupation was, however, limited to those areas considered part of greater Germany. This included Austria, parts of Hungary, and the Sudetenland in the Czech province. The kaiser refused to allow his army to get bogged down in hopeless struggles to hang onto the Balkans and Slavic east while he still faced Britain. While ethnic violence continued in the Balkans, most of the rest of the continent found itself enjoying an uneasy peace.

The diplomats talked and talked. A foundation for a future peace was hammered out, and hope that further wholesale bloodshed could be avoided began to grow. It was a false hope. The storm was building. The German production of undersea boats, or U-boats, as they were denominated, swung into high gear. The twenty-one boats Admiral Holtzendorf started with now numbered more than seventy, and new boats were being launched weekly.

The kaiser decided it was time to strike. The first fifty boats carefully and sneakily made their way through the English Channel to ports on the west coast of France. The offensive was originally scheduled to begin on June 21st, the first day of summer. It was delayed two weeks due to poor weather and logistical problems. The new date to commence hostilities was the 5th of July. On July 5th, the Germans declared an embargo on all shipping to Britain and announced they were prepared to sink any ship that ventured into British waters.

The German declaration prompted a British response in kind, that any ship, regardless of flag, bound for a port under German control would be seized or sunk. A week later, the shooting began. British losses the first day were staggering. In addition to three Royal Navy vessels, twenty-one commercial ships were lost, including the RMS *Carpathia*. While headed into the port of Southampton, she was torpedoed, caught fire, and sank less than three miles off the Isle of Wight. Only five crewmen lost their lives, and all of the passengers were saved. The spectacle of the loss of such a great symbol of British dominance of the sea was shocking. Many who had said they would never be caught dead on an airship sought the safety of the Airship America Line. After all, Britain still controlled the sky, and no submarine could touch those ships.

Owners of merchant shipping shuddered in panic. Prices for imported goods skyrocketed, and the economy of Britain slowed further. The Conservatives' gamble in turning the government over to the Liberals was about to pay off with a huge dividend. Meanwhile, the Germans showed off their new helium-filled airships by attacking Gibraltar and sinking several ships. A second squadron had attacked Suez and effectively closed the canal, creating more problems.

The new German airships were very similar to the ones they'd used before because the German factories were already producing parts, and they saw no sense in abandoning a proven design. In any event, to do so would have slowed production. The war that many hoped was nearly over flared back into existence, and the Germans had more ships in the air than did the British. The number of airships was disturbing, but by all accounts, the Germans were still well behind in their designs. They had nothing to match the new *Queen Elizabeth*. That ship and more like her, together with the rearmed Lady-class ships, gave Britain more than a fighting chance.

Now began what the papers called the air war. The RAS did not expect the Germans to be so foolish as to attack Britain directly. They were correct. The Germans continued to use their new airships to cause mischief in the Mediterranean and in the operation of the Suez Canal. From the perspective of the Admiralty, chasing around the world after individual airships seemed a pointless exercise. In her capacity as air marshal, the Duchess of Azure, Henrietta, agreed with the admirals and generals. She and the RAS needed to force the Germans to come to her. To do this, she planned to teach the Germans a lesson in humility by destroying several of their most important economic prizes. She would lead one attack deep into Germany. The Germans had anticipated the British might try something but nothing this bold.

On the night of the 16th of July, Henrietta's fleets departed. They planned to arrive by first light. Everything went according to plan. The ports of Bremerhaven and Cuxhaven were bombed. The pride of the German passenger fleet—the SS *Kaiser Wilhelm der Grosse*, SS *Kronprinze Wilhelm*, SS *Kaiser Wilhelm II*, and SS *Deutschland*—had all been hit, set on fire, and sunk. Germany had gone after a British liner in her home port. Turnabout seemed a fair response. The loss of the ships was a tremendous symbolic blow. The specter of burning ships in a supposedly safe harbor could not be hidden from the public. The smart bombs destroyed each target, and the Cimarrons pummeled the defenders with their six-pounders. By 7:00 A.M. on the morning of the 17th of July, it was over, and Henrietta and her fleet were headed home. Not a single hand had been lost. The kaiser awoke in Berlin to the news of the devastation. He was furious.

Bad weather delayed the next attack, but on the 23rd of July, the RAS struck for a second time. This attack came from the west. The new submarine bases at Brest, Lorient, and La Rochelle, France, were simultaneously struck. The British Cimarrons flew in from over the Atlantic and hit the submarines tied up at the docks. Eleven boats were lost. On the return flight, the HMA *Lady Margaretha* spotted a submarine on the surface. It dived to avoid destruction, but the *Lady Margaretha*'s captain ordered a delayed jury-rigged fuse be set on one of the small bombs he still carried aboard. It landed in the water right above the submarine and then sank to its deck before detonating. The submarine's hull was breached, it was forced to the surface, and gunfire finished it. It was the first confirmed kill of a submarine by a Cimarron.

On the floor of the House of Commons, the prime minister joked he was grateful to the kaiser for providing the Royal Air Service with submersible targets. On a more serious note, he added, "Playtime is over. It now is time to sweep every German ship from the sea." News of the prime minister's remarks reached the kaiser. This was not the commercial war he'd expected to wage. On top of that, he was losing, and he knew it. He concluded Alfred Thayer Mahon had been right all along. Mahon talked about ships because he hadn't imagined airships. The kaiser knew the nation that ruled the ocean of air rather than the waves ruled the world. If he wanted to win this war, he first needed to destroy the RAS. Predictably, the kaiser resolved to redouble his efforts.

The success of the HMA *Lady Margaretha* prompted the RAS to begin submarine patrols off the English coast. Other German submarines were spotted and driven underwater. Royal Navy destroyers would then hound the Germans to death. Tracking a submarine underwater would have been nearly impossible but for the work of a young Canadian by the name of Robert William Boyle. Building on earlier work by Jonas Lippmann and Paul Langevin, he developed and improved an underwater echo-locator for the Navy. It was difficult to operate and didn't work very well, but the clearly audible and distinctive sound it produced underwater was terrifying to submariners. When they heard it, they knew depth bombs were going to be dropped on them in the very near future. Over the next weeks, the Germans lost five more submarines, and four others were missing, listed as overdue and presumed lost.

On top of the losses was the fact that what had begun with such promise was turning into a disappointment. By the end of July, would-be targets simply waited outside Britain's territorial limit until they could be escorted in by Cimarrons and warships. The fact was, the battle space was too small to make best use of the submarine's capacity for destruction. After a month of effort, they could claim only nineteen commercial ships and five warships. In return, they had lost ten boats at sea and eleven in port. The kaiser and his admirals reasoned if the British could declare an embargo of any ship headed for a German-controlled port, they were justified in declaring they would attack ships headed to Britain. Submarines were given the unrestricted authority to attack any British ship anywhere it might be found. Militarily it was a sound decision; politically it was a disaster.

The papers in America were outraged. Then, to make matters far worse, on July 25th a German submarine captain mistook an American ship headed for Stockholm as belligerent and sank it in international waters. This time, the passengers were not so lucky. The icy waters killed 403, including 109 Americans. They included two Nobel Prize laureates and the young daughter of the American ambassador.

President Roosevelt directed the American ambassador to Berlin to inform the kaiser that if he wanted a war with America, all he need do was sink one more American ship headed to a neutral port. The kaiser had enough on his hands fighting the British RAS and realized that if America, who had invented the Cimarrons, joined the fight, his troubles would only increase. Instead of merely relying upon the submarine war to defeat Britain, the kaiser needed to end the war quickly before America could or would become involved. It was time to go back and revisit the question of how to destroy the British RAS and the Royal Navy fleet in a battle of annihilation. If he could do that, the world would be his.

The Germans are nothing if not an industrious people. Count Zeppelin and his staff had put together a significant building program before the war began. The kaiser's great ships were built well away from Britain at Friedrichshafen in far southern Germany. Located on the Swiss border, there was no way a raid wouldn't be discovered long before it arrived. The advent of special cannons that could be elevated to shoot at Cimarrons would make such a raid far too dangerous. This was particularly true given that the elevation of the surrounding area meant the Cimarrons would be flying at relatively low altitude.

Elsewhere, the kaiser kept his new airship fleet well away from the RAS. He didn't want to waste his airship fleet in pointless small battles. In any event, they had plenty of targets to the south to conduct training and to keep themselves occupied. The exception to his general rule was Berlin itself. The kaiser and the German Staff did not expect the British would try to attack Berlin. They didn't have ships to waste if a battle of annihilation was coming. Still, the kaiser kept a squadron of his airships near Berlin. He'd begun doing so right after the discovery of helium wells in East Prussia. German airships prowled overhead at all hours of the day and night. They served as a reminder to the population, and more importantly diplomats from other countries, that the sky didn't belong exclusively to the British. He wanted the world to know he and his army had a claim. The demonstrations had become so common, the population ignored the sound of engines overhead.

After the disastrous losses over London, the Germans kept building. Because of standardization of parts, airships came out of the sheds weekly. Building ships and training crews took time, but by the end of June, they had thirty-seven, or nearly three times more airships than their British rivals. The German airships appeared svelte when compared to British craft. At 780 feet in length and only 78 feet in diameter, the ships contrasted sharply with the Lady-class ships, which were 106 feet abeam, and the larger Queen class, which were 135 feet broad. With their much wider girth, "the girls" appeared sluggish and awkward.

But appearances can be deceiving. Inside the German ships was a single heavy keel along the bottom as there would be on a regular seagoing ship. The rings were then attached to this keel. The Cimarron were designed with three keels equidistant from each other, one at the top of the circle and one down each side. While each keel was lighter than the German counterpart, together they were heavier and allowed for a triangular brace between them. In addition to the triangular brace, other internal framing components were also included. This arrangement made the whole structure more robust and battle worthy.

Its heavier internal structure and great size also allowed the engines to be mounted internally. The reduction in drag and a better aerodynamic shape meant the Ladies and the Queens enjoyed a slight five-mile-per-hour speed advantage. Another noteworthy advantage gained by internal mounting of the engines was that the props on the British airship could be swiveled downward or outward, and the fifth prop could swivel through 360 degrees. No airship was nimble, but thanks to the props, the Cimarrons could change both attitude and direction comparatively quickly.

The Germans designated their new helium-filled ships with the prefix of Seiner Majestät Luftshiff, or SML. It was simply the German translation of His Majesty's Airship, or HMA, used by the British. The Germans began rebuilding their reputation as the number of ships grew. The public was told the new SML *König*, the first of the König Klasse Luftshiff, or King-class airship, was far better than the "fat" British ships. Pictures of the new Luftshiffe began appearing in newspapers. Some of these pictures made their way to Britain. The new German ship's vastly improved engines were still housed in nacelles outside of the hull. This had originally been done as a fire-preventive measure when hydrogen was used. The design was retained because it worked well with other design components, but it made the engines a more visible target.

Apart from speed, strength, and grace, the Cimarrons of the RAS enjoyed a tremendous advantage in armaments. The Germans opted to use a 50 mm/40 cannon originally developed to arm torpedo boats. They also had tried mounting heavier guns, but the lower rate of fire and excessive weight of the system were incompatible with their needs. The 50 mm/40 was lighter than the Mark III QF six-pounder Hotchkiss guns the RAS employed over London, and it had a good rate of fire at twenty rounds per minute. As good a weapon as it was, it did not compare to the new 40 mm heavy machine gun the RAS now relied on. The Anglo-American, or AA, weapon boasted the same range and a rate of fire six times greater. The existence of the 40 mm AA gun was a closely guarded secret.

Plans to take the war to the RAS and finish it once and for all began in earnest. While the British press persisted in calling the Duchess of Azure the Queen of the Sky, the kaiser had several of his own names for her. The only one that could be repeated in polite company was "Amerikanische Hexe," or "American witch." He called his generals in and demanded a plan. The result was a simple and straightforward operation to overwhelm the British by sheer weight of numbers, even trading ships, two or three to one. the arithmetic was undeniable and gave the Germans the advantage.

The kaiser set the date for the attack as August 14th or as soon thereafter as weather permitted. It was all going well, but what the kaiser had not counted on was the pluck and ingenuity of the RAS and their American witch. She and her forces were about to change the math.

Chapter Thirteen:
Midnight Surprise

Back on the first of July, Flight Leader John Jeter presented an idea to the air marshal and the air vice marshal. It was something the SAS had come up with on its own. Jeter began, "The biggest virtue of this idea is no one has ever tried it before, so no one will be expecting it."

"What is it?"

"It is a clandestine SAS operation targeting the kaiser to put an end to the war."

"It sounds crazy."

"Let me explain. If we can make it work, it will end the war with a minimum of casualties."

Henrietta wanted to hear more, so she baited him. "What are you not telling me? Could it be that if we fail, we will likely make matters worse and get everyone involved killed?"

Not to be dissuaded so easily, Jeter shook his head and explained, "Your Grace, by all accounts, Kaiser Wilhelm II is the single person most responsible for the continuation of the war. As you know, he has set Germany on what he calls 'the new course.' He has always been jealous of his British relatives, including the king. He doesn't want to just build a navy to rival the Royal Navy. What he really wants is to rival Britain as a world power. For him, it is not just about ships and armies; it is about building a German empire. As long as he is in command, the war will continue. We propose to take him out of the equation."

Henrietta listened and then said, "Mr. Jeter, neither the king nor I wish to see the kaiser killed, so the answer is no."

"Begging your pardon, Your Grace, we are not proposing we kill him—not at all. We have something else in mind."

"I'm listening."

"We propose we capture him."

"Where? How?"

"We originally thought about trying to get him in the fall. He likes to go hunting in East Prussia. He and his whole entourage go. Typically, they stay for weeks. This year, he is planning to make the trip, but if the war isn't over, he won't. East Prussia is too far away from the action.

"If not East Prussia, where?"

"Berlin. The Imperial Palace, to be precise."

"How are you going to do that? Just fly down and scoop him up?"

"Exactly. We want to send a team in by parachute, capture him, and then lift him out on a boatswain's chair."

"Mr. Jeter, that is crazy. There will be guards."

"Yes, some…but in the middle of the night, they'll be half asleep, if they are not completely asleep."

Flight Lieutenant James (Jimmy) Hardcastle interjected, "From what we know, there will be only forty men and three officers. More importantly, they will be standing guard, watching for trouble on the streets. They won't be looking up. If we come in and jump from twelve hundred feet, we'll be on them before they know what is happening."

After hearing the details, Henrietta was still not convinced. "Gentlemen, I do not pretend to be an expert on parachutes, but I can see several flaws in your plan. To make it work, the Cimarron must get to Berlin without being discovered. Then we have to fly precisely above the target and pray there is no wind if you are to have any hope of landing where you want to."

"In the still of the night, that shouldn't be a problem."

"There generally is still some wind, even on a calm night. That there will be no wind at all is too much to hope for. If you want to try this, first you must find a better way to make sure the men can get exactly where they need to be."

Air Vice Marshal Wilkinson, who had been sitting silently, then added, "On top of that, if there is any shooting, the whole city will be alerted. Who knows how many might respond to that?"

Henrietta finished the meeting, saying, "If you want to proceed with this crazy idea, find answers to those problems and then bring it back to us."

The idea of capturing the kaiser was still enticing even though the idea of parachuting in was rejected. The SAS men went back and tried to figure out the answers they needed. Flight Lieutenant Jimmy Hardcastle suggested, "We could just slide down ropes." He wasn't joking. He'd been climbing in the Alps on several occasions and had learned a technique of controlled descent of a vertical rock face using a rope known as *abseiling* in German and *rappelling* in French. He suggested a team might quickly descend from a Cimarron to a precise landing point. This idea had some potential. No one would leave the Cimarron without knowing where he or she would land. Henrietta agreed to test the idea. Several landings from the HMA *Lady Alice* proved it worked.

The next problem was that the Cimarron's engines would make noise. Jeter reported, "An American by the name of Milton Reeves gave us the ideal solution. He calls his invention a *muffler*. It is a kind of silencer that he installs on automobiles and motorcycles and makes them quieter."

Henrietta liked the idea and had the Cimarron Airship Company engineers go to work on it. They built silencers for all engines. Each device had a series of baffles lined with wire wool. The design broke up exhaust gas and trapped much of the noise produced by escaping steam. The mufflers did have a drawback. They created back pressure in the engines and dramatically reduced the power output along with the sound. The answer came once again from Mr. Jeter. He suggested, "We could just use the silencers for final approach to the target. The engineers tell us that by adding a bypass pipe, full power can be restored by simply opening a valve." It was all very clever.

The last problem was all the racket any gunfire would make. Air Vice Marshal Wilkinson commented, "All right, you can get troops onto the ground, but the surprise is going to be lost the moment the shooting starts. Everyone will know you're there and up to something. What do you propose to avoid that?

Flight Leader Percival Heathcliff Montgomery (Percy to all who knew him) said, "We've thought of that too. We've been looking at weapons. The lads have come up with several weapons."

"What did they find?"

Percy said, "The most remarkable weapon we've found so far is the Nagant M1895 revolver with a Maxim silencer."

Henrietta asked, "And what is that?"

"It is a pistol designed by a Belgian by the name of Leon Nagant. His brother designed the Russian army rifle the Mosin-Negant. Leon's pistol is now the standard sidearm to the Imperial Russian Army."

"What is remarkable about that?"

"It is kind of complicated."

Henrietta looked at Percy as if he were speaking Martian. Icily, she said, "I realize I am only a woman, but I think if you explain it slowly, I will be able to understand."

Percy was stunned by the response and stammered, "I beg your pardon, Your Grace. I didn't mean to imply that you wouldn't understand.…I am so…"

Henrietta laughed. "Relax, Percy. I'm just teasing you. Please tell me about the gun and the silencer."

Now embarrassed, Percy shook it off and smiled. "Your Grace, the pistol has a unique design feature. When it is cocked, the cylinder moves forward and seals the chamber with the bullet to the barrel. In most pistols, there is a gap, and some of the hot gas from the burning powder escapes. It makes noise. The M1895 doesn't let that happen. The gas from the burnt powder all comes out of the end of the barrel. A young man named H. P. Maxim created a device that reduces the sound of that escaping gas."

"Is this man Maxim somehow connected to the Maxim gun?"

"Yes. He's the son of Hiram Maxim, the man who came up with the machine gun."

"Tell me more about this silencer."

"Back in 1902, the boy came up with it. It looks like a short section of pipe on the end of the barrel. When it is attached, it makes a gun quiet."

"So, if you use these, no one will hear the shooting?"

"Not exactly. It isn't truly silent, but the noise it makes is barely audible and would never be recognized as gunfire."

"That sounds very promising."

Encouraged, Percy continued, "The thing is, we've been working on rifles with the same setup."

"Tell me about them."

"We started out with an American-made 44-40 caliber lever-action rifle, then added a silencer. A good shot can hit a man easily at 150 yards if they have a Kahles—that's an Austrian-made hunting telescopic sight. Shots of four hundred yards or more are possible. We even made up a shortened version of the rifle to use inside buildings."

"Is it still effective?"

"Very much so. The weapon, silencer and all, is less than three feet long, but with a twelve-inch barrel and a six-inch silencer, you can swing it around inside a room. At one hundred yards you can't miss hitting a man."

Further discussion followed, but it was clear that the crazy idea would work if surprise could be maintained. Preparation for the kidnapping began in earnest. The best time would be a moonless night. The next was to occur on July 31st. The hope was that without a moon to give them away, the landings would come as a complete surprise. HMA *Queen Elizabeth* would fly into Germany after dark and make her way to Berlin. On board would be two platoons of sixteen men each for a total of thirty-two. One platoon would remain aboard and provide covering rifle fire and reinforcement for the other platoon. The landing platoon would rappel down to the palace's central courtyard. Four members of the platoon would remain in the courtyard and prepare for the kaiser's extraction. The rest of the platoon would rush into the private apartment of the Imperial Palace and capture the kaiser. Once he was secured, he would be taken to the courtyard and lifted out on a boatswain's chair. When the kaiser was safely aboard, the platoon was to be lifted out on special lines that allowed several men to be hoisted together.

When all was in place, HMA *Queen Elizabeth* would begin her mission. The date of the operation was beyond top secret, so Henrietta could not tell Connie. She did talk to him in general terms about what they were "thinking about trying." She began, "Because I am air marshal, I must go along and be in personal command of the operation."

He asked, "Why on Earth would that be necessary? Isn't it too risky a mission for you as the head of the RAS to chance?"

"Because if it all goes wrong, someone will need to take the blame. That someone has to be me. If I'm there, it is a military operation, and the others can't be accused of being assassins or spies operating on their own."

"Couldn't your vice air marshal go instead? I mean, he is a military man after all."

"He could, but if things go wrong, I know how you gentlemen are. Once you get it in your head to do something, you'll push ahead no matter what the odds."

"You don't trust him?"

"No, the problem is that I do. If I give an order to do it, he'll do it or die trying. If this turns out to be a trap, I can put a halt to it; the others won't disobey me."

Henrietta believed getting into Germany and even to Berlin was not going to be a big problem. They just needed to be careful and not get caught. Getting out would be a whole different matter, particularly if the entire German Empire was alert and trying to stop them. That would be when it could all go wrong and might even require surrender.

The night of the operation was perfect—mostly cloudy with a chance of late-night rain. Just after dark, HMA *Queen Elizabeth* crossed the German coast south of the border with Denmark. It was a relatively sparsely populated area. Flying at flank speed, she reached the Baltic Sea undetected. Flying east-southeast over the water, she flew to a point on the North German coast less than two hundred miles from Berlin. She then turned south, heading toward the capital. By staying above five thousand feet, the sound of the airship's engines did not raise an alarm.

As the ship approached the lights of Berlin, Captain Truscott gave the order to slow down and engage the silencers. The sound that reached the ground made it seem as if she were just another German airship conducting night maneuvers off in the distance. The great airship slipped through the dark, cloudy sky until at last she was only three miles from the Imperial Palace. The breeze was a slight four miles per hour from the west. The *Queen* slowed further and began to descend until she was creeping ahead, dead slow, at one thousand feet relative altitude.

The bridge of the *Queen Elizabeth* was different from the one on Lady-class ships. The Queen-class ships were designed from the outset to serve as flagships, so the control cabin was larger. Immediate control of flight operations was the same as on the Ladies. Helm's station was still at the very front of the cabin; Flight was still to the left and Props to the right. It was one step down from the command chair located in the middle of the bridge. Navigation and Guns were at the same level behind the command chair. Both stations had been enlarged and a second command chair installed on a raised step in the center. It was called "the air marshal's perch." As befitted her station, the air marshal's perch was a high-back swivel chair that did not allow others to look over her shoulder. From it, Henrietta could keep an eye on her own airship and the others in the area. Henrietta and Captain Truscott still sat close enough to each other that they could speak directly if need be without involving the others.

Captain Truscott stood and walked to the window to get a better view of the ground. He ordered, "Helm, steady up, and let the wind take us into position. Keep her nose in wind. Props, stand by to back engines. I want to stop us just short of fully over the target."

Guns called out, "Thirty seconds."

Captain Truscott ordered, "Give us a countdown."

Henrietta sat silently. She'd done all she could. Now she had to sit and watch the plan unfold. She prayed that it would be successful. When the SAS had put the plan forward, she had insisted every aspect be researched and rehearsed. The interior layout of the German Imperial Palace was not a secret. Over the years, British visitors had built up a clear picture of the building's interior.

Various alternative routes by which the assault team could reach the royal apartment were discussed. In the end, one route was settled on as being the least difficult. The team expected to encounter sentries at the doors and perhaps at two or three other locations inside. As air marshal, Henrietta had been able to "borrow" a large manor house in the Midlands. Adjacent to it were several relatively large stone outbuildings, including a carriage house with a walled horse paddock. The dimensions of the space between them matched those of the courtyard of the German Imperial Palace. It was an ideal site to conduct dress rehearsals of the landings, and the house was ideal to practice running upstairs at night and dealing with guards. After two weeks of hard training, everyone felt comfortable they knew what was expected.

The final minutes ticked away as Helm brought the ship to a stop just as would be done when mooring. Once in position, Captain Truscott said softly, "We're here."

That was the signal Henrietta had been waiting for. She gave the order: "Start operational timer. Begin on my mark…Mark!"

Guns flipped a switch. Green lights came on in the bay where the assault teams waited and at several other locations where men with silenced rifles watched. Within seconds, the sentries in the courtyard lay dead on the ground, shot by silenced rifles. Ropes dropped out of the airship, and the assault team landed. Two sentries who had been under cover to stay out of the rain emerged to see what was happening. They died in a hail of silenced gunfire.

The assault team rushed into the building, pistols drawn. They encountered six more individuals. The silenced guns whispered, and the men died. The four-man entry team reached the door to the royal apartment. The two sentries standing guard were shot down. The team stepped over the bodies and into the interior of the first room. The door to the bedroom in which the kaiser slept was closed. Opening it quietly, they found him still asleep. Flight Leader Jeter, the leader of the team, placed his gloved hand securely over the kaiser's mouth, waking him with a start. Softly in German, he said, "We are not here to kill you. We are taking you prisoner. Do not cry out or raise an alarm, and you will not be injured. Do you understand?"

The kaiser's eyes opened wide, and he nodded his head in agreement.

"We are British soldiers." Flight Leader Jeter pointed at his armband. It was a Union Jack. "You are our prisoner. I'm going to take my hand away. No sound or you will be injured."

The kaiser strained to see exactly what was going on. There were at least three other men in the room, each with similar armbands, and all of them had guns.

"You are coming with us," said Jeter. "I am going to gag you now. It is for your own protection."

The kaiser could see there was no point in resisting. If there was to be an assassination, he'd be dead already. He decided to let himself be taken.

The group ran through the building to the courtyard. Four more individuals who came to investigate were shot down before the boatswain's chair carried the kaiser into the air. Within a minute, all sixteen members of the assault force had attached themselves to lines, and the great airship was pulling them up. Amazingly, there had been no casualties among the assault team.

The *Queen Elizabeth* disappeared into the clouds. Henrietta, on receiving confirmation the kaiser was aboard, said, "Captain, let's go home."

Captain Truscott gave the orders. "Navigation, give us a heading to coast. Flight, take us up to five thousand. Props, ahead full."

The silencers were disengaged, and the engines sprang to life. At 4,500 feet, the airship broke through the top of the cloud cover. It was a dark but beautiful night. At five thousand feet, the clouds, just five hundred feet below them, looked like the calm ocean. The Cimarron sped north at flank speed. Part of the plan was to rendezvous with several other British airships waiting for them over the Baltic.

It hadn't taken the Germans long to figure out what had happened. Terrified servants had watched the SAS troops in the courtyard. They'd seen them place the kaiser in a boatswain's chair and be hoisted. They had then stared in awe as the troops were lifted out nearly at once. The sound of the engines that followed left no doubt.

Within minutes, the army reacted and called the airfield just to the west of Berlin. German airships were in pursuit within thirty minutes. In the twilight of the dawn, the aft lookout aboard HMA *Queen Elizabeth* sighted a dark, barely visible shape far to the south. As the sun rose, the mighty Cimarron pulled away, and the image disappeared. It was a safe bet they were being chased. If they slowed at all, they would be overtaken.

Aboard, all remained quiet but alert to the danger. The kaiser had been taken to the air marshal's cabin. The officers who accompanied him had orders to treat him as a very special guest.

"Sir, we realize we took you from your bed, still in your bedclothes. As you didn't have time to dress, perhaps you'd like to get cleaned up and dressed now?"

"Where am I?"

"You are aboard His Majesty's Airship *Queen Elizabeth*."

"But..."

"It will all be explained to you by our commander. You'll need to get cleaned up and dressed first."

"Cleaned up? Dressed?"

"Yes sir. There is a private bath off of this cabin, and we've brought several uniforms that we believe will fit you."

"But how...?"

"We did some work with a tailor on Savile Row."

"But tell me..."

"I'm sorry, sir, but explanations will need to come from the commander."

Still full of questions, the kaiser gave in. He got cleaned up and dressed. He was sitting having a cup of coffee when a young officer stuck his head in. It was still very early.

"Is he ready to receive company?"

"I believe so."

A moment later, the door opened, and Henrietta stepped into the room. "Your Imperial and Royal Majesty, allow me to introduce our commander, Air Marshal, the Duchess of Azure."

Henrietta curtseyed. After all, he was a blood royal, even if he was her prisoner.

The kaiser gasped as she rose. "You!"

"Yes, it is I."

"What is the meaning of this, this, this…?"

"Sir, I have taken you prisoner in an effort to find a way to end the war between your nation and mine."

"But—"

"We took you, and now we are on our way to London. I intend to take you to His Majesty so the two of you may settle this dispute."

"And what if I refuse?"

"It will be up to His Majesty what is to become of you." Henrietta smiled. "I am sure you have many questions. Please sit down and ask me whatever you'd like."

They sat. "Tell me, young lady, what my uncle thinks he's going to achieve."

"Sir, I don't think you understand. His Majesty had nothing to do with this. I have done this on my own. He will be told you are on your way when he rises."

"Without his—?"

Henrietta felt the great Cimarron turn hard. The sudden motion stopped the kaiser. Before he could finish, a young officer stuck his head in and said, "I beg your pardon."

"What is it, Mr. Mathers?"

"Air Marshal, the captain says we have company and asks that you come to the bridge."

Henrietta's smile left her face. "Very well, Mr. Mathers. Sir, you must forgive me. Duty calls, and I'm afraid we'll have to continue this later." She stood and walked out. As she walked, the alarm blared. It called the crew to battle stations.

On Henrietta reaching the bridge, Captain Truscott said, "Your Grace, we may have a fight on our hands."

"Report."

"Lookouts spotted an airship off our port bow. It's twenty thousand yards off but appears to be bearing on us and driving hard."

"Where did she come from?"

"She came out of the broken clouds at four thousand feet."

"Can you tell what she is?"

"Hard to say, but she's German, and she's big. She's got six engines. We estimate her speed at better than eighty miles per hour."

Henrietta said softly, "My word, that is fast." Then shaking her head, she swallowed hard. The last thing she wanted was an air battle over Germany. Setting her jaw, she said, "It doesn't matter. With the pursuer behind us, we can't evade and run. We'll have to get past her if we are to get to the coast. How much time do we have?"

Captain Truscott answered, "I turned the ship and bought us what time I could." Over his shoulder, he asked, "Guns, how long until intercept?"

Guns answered, "Five minutes to range."

Henrietta paused, then said, "It is clear they know where we are. No sense in staying off the radio. Signal our escort and tell them what is happening. Gentlemen, ladies, it appears we will be fighting this morning. Mr. Mathers, go back and get the kaiser fitted with a parachute. We're responsible for his safety now."

Turning back to the captain, Henrietta asked, "Mr. Truscott, the *Queen Elizabeth* is your ship. How do you propose to fight?"

"I think we wait and make a turn to bring our guns to bear when she's just coming into range. With luck, we'll force the Germans to fly into them or turn and fight at range."

"I agree. I was thinking the same thing. Give the orders."

Captain Truscott issued the commands. "Guns, call the distance by thousands until we reach ten thousand yards, then by hundreds. Tell your crews we'll commence fire at the turn."

"Call by thousands to ten, then by hundreds. Fire on the turn, aye."

"Helm, we turn to starboard at eight thousand yards. Once we've moved enough to clear the guns, we turn back to our heading." After taking a breath, Truscott went on. "Props, we'll remain at full ahead until the turn. Be alert. As we turn, I'm going to want to put on the brakes on our starboard side so we turn as fast as possible. As soon as we are clear, I'll order us back to emergency ahead."

Helm answered, "Turn at eight thousand till the guns clear, aye."

Props added, "Standing by to reverse starboard thrust at the turn, then emergency ahead, aye."

Henrietta was grateful Captain Truscott was there to give orders. Her mouth was so dry, she wasn't sure if she could. This was going to be a hard fight. This German ship was so much bigger and better than those she had fought over London. The fight would take much longer, and this time there would be casualties. Still, there was no way to avoid it. No matter how terrible it was going to be, this battle had to be fought.

The German commander aboard the SML *Leopold* appeared to have the same idea as Captain Truscott. He began his turn just moments before the *Queen Elizabeth*. The 50 mm cannons flashed. Most of the shells passed harmlessly through the Cimarron, but one round hit the forward engine room. It exploded and destroyed the boiler for the portside engine. A second round hit just behind the bridge. When it exploded, the crewmen and crewwomen in the navigation station were killed instantly. Henrietta escaped injury only because she had turned her chair away to speak to Guns, and the seat back and her parachute absorbed the blast and flying debris. Her chair, like all of the others on the bridge, had been reinforced to provide at least some protection. Captain Truscott was not so lucky. He was struck on the side of his head and knocked unconscious. He was carried from the bridge with blood flowing from a gash on his scalp.

Henrietta now took personal command. The first officer and the navigator, who was second officer, were both dead. Gunners on the *Queen* fired back with their AA guns. In moments, the bridge of the German ship was a mass of torn metal, and the forward gas bags were in tatters. The three engine nacelles visible on the German airship's port side had all been hit and the engines put out of action. With the German captain killed, the engines on the starboard side received no orders to stop and continued to run. Down by the bow, the power to the starboard side pushed the German ship until her mass masked her primary guns. The *Queen*'s engineers adjusted her props and kept her on course and her guns bearing. The gunners on top of the German airship did not give up. They fired heavy machine guns at the Britons. They caused some damage but nothing serious. *Queen*'s gunners found the range and were tearing the German airship apart. Shell after shell tore away parts of the enemy craft. The German ship rolled, and one of her guns cleared and began firing. A lucky shot killed the gun crew manning the *Queen*'s number two mount. A second shot damaged the number four engine beyond repair.

It was too little too late. The German airship was doomed. The British responded with dozens of 40 mm shells raking through the German airship from bow to stern. The German guns fell silent. Somewhere deep inside her, a magazine exploded. The ship's back broken, she started to settle to the ground.

The *Queen Elizabeth* limped away. As badly wounded as she was, she was not dead, at least not yet. Two of her five engines were damaged beyond repair and three of her gun mounts destroyed. Eight of the crew were dead and twelve others seriously wounded. Still half deaf from the explosion on the bridge, Henrietta surveyed the situation. The injured were moved, and other crewmen took their places. "Flight report."

"The outer rings five, six, and eight are all damaged, and number seven has a twenty-foot gap. The internal bracing is holding us together, but we are losing lift. I've dropped all of the water ballast, and I've got crews working on repairing the bags. We should be able to stay airborne if we don't run into trouble again."

"Guns, what about the Germans?"

"We were about twenty minutes ahead of the pursuit. Still no sign of them, but I am assuming they stayed after us."

"Props?"

"We lost engines one and four, but two, three, and five are all at full power. We can still make fifty or better."

"Give me what you can. Maybe with luck we'll be able to reach the coast before they overtake us."

One hundred twenty miles to the north, the crews aboard HMA *Queen Victoria*, HMA *Lady Jane*, and HMA *Lady Beatrice* heard the news. Henrietta had the kaiser but was going to be in a fight before they could get there to help. When word of the battle reached them and they learned the *Queen Elizabeth* was hurt, they knew what they had to do. With daylight, the Germans also knew exactly where HMA *Queen Elizabeth* was.

The race was on. In just under an hour, the British ships sighted one another. The trailing German airship was charging hard in hopes of catching the Britons before help arrived but was too late. The German commander knew his ship could not hope to match the four British airships even if one was wounded. The commander pulled up short and began shadowing them. He radioed his position. The General Staff in Berlin decided they would try to bring down the British when they turned west and headed for England. The radio and telegraph spread the word. Eleven German Luftshiffe massed south of Denmark.

Then Henrietta did the unthinkable. She did not turn. Ignoring Danish neutrality, she flew north-northwest across Denmark. The German Luftshiff captain had orders not to violate Danish neutrality. As the British flew on, he slowed, waiting for direction from Berlin. By the time he got authorization to proceed, the British were more than an hour away and had changed course, making pursuit virtually impossible. Henrietta did not turn west until they reached the North Sea. Flying zigzag over that trackless ocean, the Germans searched but would never find them.

Once the *Queen Elizabeth* had her escort, Henrietta returned to the kaiser. "I'm glad to see you are all right."

"I heard all of the firing earlier. What happened?"

"One of your airships intercepted us."

"I knew they would not let you get away with this."

"We shot it down."

"Shot it down?"

Henrietta lied. "It wasn't really much of a contest. We are leaving Germany. It will take us the rest of the day and most of the night, but by morning, we will be in London."

"They'll stop you."

"No, I do not think so. We are not alone."

"Not alone?"

"If you will come with me, I'll show you."

Henrietta took the kaiser down the hall to the main observation lounge. She pointed to the window. "Take a look."

The kaiser looked out, and his heart sank. He could see the three British Cimarrons holding station. He began to get angry. "I don't know who you think you are, but you will pay for this, you—"

Henrietta was not about to let anyone speak as he was about to. She spoke to him as a mother might scold a child. "Now, none of that. Manners, if you please. You are my guest and should behave like a gentleman." The sternness in her voice left the kaiser with no doubt. He figuratively bit his lip and remained silent. "I have many things to do today," said Henrietta, "but if you give me your word to behave, you may stay here in the observation area and watch our progress. A little later, I will take you on a tour of this ship."

A curt "thank you" was the kaiser's only response.

Henrietta finished by saying, "Now you will have to excuse me again. I must return to my duties. Flight Leader Jeter and Flying Officer Hardcastle will remain with you and see to your needs. I will let you know when we are ready for the tour. After it is over, we can sit down and have a proper meal together. Rest assured, we will try to make your stay with us as comfortable as possible."

By noon, the *Queen Elizabeth* was well north of Copenhagen. Among the airship's crew were several who knew how to cook. The result was that the food aboard the *Queen Elizabeth* was noticeably better than one might expect on a warship. Henrietta had made it a point to find out the kaiser's favorite dishes. Having a formal luncheon with a beautiful and gracious hostess was hardly what he expected. Henrietta had several of her officers join them. Her aides-de-camp Flight Leader Theodore Pierce and Flying Officer Lidya Ives joined them. Mr. Pierce was an avid hunter, and Lidya spoke fluent German.

Talk around the table was surprisingly relaxed. Henrietta had her mother to thank for the art of talking to anyone. She complimented the kaiser on the effectiveness of the German Army and agreed that it was only proper for such a great nation to be recognized as a true world leader. He thanked her and agreed. Then to his surprise, she went on, "It is truly unfair, for want of a better term, that my British cousins look down upon the Germans and treat you so unfairly." To his surprise, he agreed with Henrietta again. She went on, saying, "As a woman, I have a somewhat different view of unfair treatment than some of my countrymen. I believe nations as well as individuals should have a level field to play upon. I am not certain that has been the case with Germany."

"I'm not certain Britain and Germany could get along."

"Why not? People from England and from Germany get along in America. In fact, my very best friend in the world is Baroness Margaretha Von-Kleist. If we can get along, I think if you and the king, especially as relatives, should be able to sit down and together decide what is really important. I think you might be surprised by what is possible if further bloodshed can be avoided." The kaiser listened in silence, so she continued, "I am not the one to ask, but I can say as a student of history that Britain's fought more wars with France than anyone else. It would appear to me France is Britain's natural enemy, not Germany."

"Young lady, you really are full of surprises."

"Thank you."

By the end of the meal, the kaiser was not fully convinced but had to admit just how remarkable the Duchess of Azure was. She'd kidnapped him, but despite himself, he began to admire her and, truth be known, like her.

Word of the kaiser's abduction was kept hidden from the public. The German military was mortified. Their leader had been taken right under their noses. To admit it would be humiliating. A cover story about an assassination attempt was used to explain the kaiser's sudden disappearance. There were too many witnesses to the airship over Berlin and the subsequent fight between the SML *Leopold* and the HMA *Queen Elizabeth* for the matter to be ignored. By midday, the rumor had started that the kaiser was dead. The gossip prompted all sorts of speculation in the press. Across the Channel in England, word of the battle between HMA *Queen Elizabeth* and SML *Leopold* had reached London. It too started a second rumor that the kaiser had been deposed.

When the *Queen Elizabeth* arrived, Connie was the first person to greet Henrietta. "You lunatic! What did you think you were doing running off like that and not telling me?! You could have been killed!"

"Oh, Connie, dear…" The rest of her answer was smothered by a long, passionate kiss.

The problem with making up a cover story in a hurry is that it is too easy to get tripped up. By day's end, Britain and the world were ablaze with the news that the Queen of the Sky had swooped down and stolen the kaiser right out of his bedroom. As the situation threatened to get out of hand, the British government opted to lie to the press. The newspapers were told the kaiser was indeed alive and would be paying a surprise visit to London. They even went so far as to say he was travelling by Cimarron as a show of good faith that his was a mission of peace.

Hurriedly, a formal ceremony was arranged. The kaiser was greeted at the Royal Pavilion at Horse Guards Parade. An honor guard gave him a royal salute, he reviewed the troops, and the German national anthem was played. He and the king then rode by carriage to Buckingham Palace for talks.

When first they met, the kaiser protested to the king of his abduction by Henrietta and the SAS. The king just chuckled. "What did you expect? You said some very unkind things about the good air marshal, the Duchess of Azure, and you made her mad. I suggest that whatever else you do, you don't repeat that mistake here. No telling what she might do." That silenced the kaiser. The king added softly, "We will speak privately when the ceremony is over. Save your complaints until then."

What the two men actually spoke about would never be fully revealed, but one fact did emerge. The trip on the *Queen Elizabeth* with Henrietta had convinced the kaiser he'd been deluding himself. German airships were no match for those of the British and Americans.

The politicians sent Henrietta dozens of radio messages as she had traveled home. They wanted her to tell the newspapers the story they'd concocted. When she arrived, they asked if she would comply with their requests. Henrietta curtly responded, "I refuse to lie to the press."

"You have to say something. What will you say?"

"I will say only that the kaiser was a welcome guest on my Cimarron."

"What if they want to know how he got aboard?"

"I will say it was by boatswain's chair similar to the one I have used myself."

"They will want details."

"Wanting and getting are two different things. I will say that for security reasons, I am not prepared to discuss details of how the Royal Air Service conducts operations."

"Don't you think they will object?"

"Of course they will object. I'm confident they won't like it one bit, but it won't be a lie, and it will be all they get from me."

In the end, it was the wise heads in the British Foreign Office and the German Chancellery that saved the day. They saw the whole affair as just what was needed to find an excuse to end the war on acceptable terms to both sides. Aside from Britain's overwhelming desire to preserve its empire, it had two primary concerns. First was to steadfastly oppose Russian expansion, and second was to pacify Britain's age-old enemy, France. Germany shared two of the same concerns. They were anxious to discourage Russian meddling and wished to prevent the reemergence of France as a military threat. They had no real desire to threaten Britain's empire, but they did want an empire of their own.

The commonality of concerns opened the way for a new understanding between the powers and the formation of the Council of Nations. Germany was to withdraw from Belgium and cease its effort to challenge Britain's dominance at sea. The basic terms of an arms limitation treaty were hammered out. In exchange, Britain would agree to Germany's disarming France and keeping much of the French colonial empire for itself. Britain and its ally Japan would acquire a few bits of the old French empire as an incentive to participate in the scheme. Britain would take over the island of Madagascar, and Japan would take over French Indochina. Germany would keep all of the other colonies, giving the kaiser the empire he wanted. It was understood each empire would enjoy a degree of free reign within their respective areas of concern. This would leave Germany free to deal with Russia and the chaos that was sweeping through the Balkans, Britain free to contest the Middle East, and Japan to hold the Far East.

The Danes filed a formal protest over Henrietta's action in disregarding their neutrality, but when it brought an end to the war and hope for a lasting peace, they withdrew it. The Americans were appalled but were told they had chosen neutrality and isolationism so had no say in the matter. They were placated when they were told that the three powers had agreed to a protocol that recognized the United States was to be treated as a fourth informal but coequal member of the Council of Nations. The French protested vehemently but were told that if they did not agree, their country would be permanently partitioned and pieces given to Britain, Germany, Spain, and Italy. While it didn't silence the French, it allowed for the end to the occupation by the German Army. These arrangements would not make the three principal powers formal allies, but it would make them more than friends and keep them out of conflict with each other.

Chapter Fourteen: New Adventures

Now riding a wave of popularity, Britain's Liberal government called for elections, and it looked like the Conservatives' gamble wasn't going to pay off after all. While the end of the war brought peace, it did not bring an end to Henrietta's struggles.

The Duchess of Azure was someone whom virtually everyone admired and many wished to emulate. All sides saw her as the perfect symbol for their agenda. The Conservatives were quick to point out it was they who had originally empowered her to save Britain, and she was born into the aristocracy. Lord Palmer had become a close friend, and the former prime minister liked her. The Liberals pointed to her recent victory and her treatment of her staff and employees. Henrietta begged them all to leave her out of it. She pleaded, "I am a serving officer in His Majesty's forces. I cannot and will not become involved in politics."

That placated most of them but not the suffragettes. They were bound and determined to get her involved in their movement. They found an old newspaper account of Henrietta's humorous answer to a reporter's question perfect for their needs. When asked about votes for women, Henrietta had quipped, "Sir, I am not a political person, but I do consider women every bit as capable as men, except in matters of childbirth, at which we excel and at which men are at a disadvantage." Every pamphlet and flyer produced by the suffragettes prominently included some part of the quotation. Soon signs began appearing at rallies demanding the Duchess of Azure run for Parliament and even for prime minister. It emphasized that even so great a lady and peer as she was, she was still a second-class citizen, a mere woman unable to vote or participate in either the House of Lords or the House of Commons.

Henrietta complained bitterly to her fiancé, Connie. "This is much worse than having all the young men in Britain after me to marry them. Now it is women."

"Ah, the price of fame and folly. Don't you want to be a suffragette?"

"No, I do not want to be a suffragette. Some of those girls are crazy. I'd rather take my chances getting shot at in a battle than put up with all of their nonsense."

"That's not very gracious."

"But it's true."

"Then you need to tell them you are content to have women treated as second-class citizens and do not want them to have the vote."

"That's not true, and you know it."

"Then demand the vote and run to pick up a banner."

"Harrumph! You're no help!"

Connie took Henrietta in his arms. "Then tell them you are so much in love, all you can think about is me." He kissed her.

As he pulled back, she smiled. "I like the way you are thinking. Still, as much fun as that sounds, I don't think it would work."

"Then we must find some other way to get you away from them. Maybe you could run away?"

"I don't run away."

"No, I don't mean run away; I mean get away."

"What are you talking about?"

"You've always said you want to explore the world. Why not take the *Queen Elizabeth* on a goodwill tour of the empire for our honeymoon? We can go to all the places you've ever dreamed of."

"You want to go on a world tour?"

"We just need to make sure we're gone when the election takes place."

"Well, there are a few places on this planet I'd like to visit."

"Then after the ceremony, we will take our leave and depart."

After the end of the war, Henrietta's admirers hoped her wedding would be a spectacular state event. They were not disappointed. Henrietta and Coinneach knew they could not escape the limelight. Every time that they went anywhere, Henrietta was mobbed. She gave in to the pressure and agreed the wedding should be held at St. Clement Danes in London. During the Battle of London, a stray incendiary shell fired by HMA *Lady Cimarron* had struck the church and set it on fire. The fire service had managed to save the building, but it was severely damaged. Lady Henrietta felt bad if not responsible. She paid for the restoration herself and was honored with a statue in front of the building. It became the spiritual home of the Royal Air Service. And it was the perfect venue for her wedding.

Following the ceremony, there was a motorcade to the reception, which was held, in a break from tradition, at Buckingham Palace. The happy couple stayed at the palace on their wedding night, and after lunching with the king and queen, they left for the HMA *Queen Elizabeth*, moored at Osterley Manor Air Terminal. After last-minute preparations were completed, the good ship departed just after dusk. Where it was headed was not announced and was known only to the RAS, the Admiralty, and a few knowledgeable individuals within the government. The plan was for a tour around the world that would take nearly six weeks.

As they stood looking out the window in the air marshal's newly renovated private cabin, Henrietta and Connie could see the lights of London. Connie asked, "Have you ever considered what the world would be like without you?"

"Without me?"

"Yes."

"Not really. I guess it would be pretty much the same."

"Are you kidding? After all you've done? You're the Queen of the Sky, or haven't you heard?"

"I didn't do that much."

"I beg to differ. Because you were there, the *Lady Cimarron* didn't crash into the sea, and transatlantic airship travel became a reality. Just imagine if that had happened, we would have had to rely on people like those brothers in Ohio to get people into the air."

"They built a heavier-than-air flying machine."

Walking across the cabin, Connie picked up a copy of a magazine. On the front cover was a picture of the Wright Flyer. Showing it to Henrietta, he said, "If you can call a ride on a kite with a motor on it flying."

"It's a start."

"I don't think going all of twenty-four miles on a closed course at thirty-six miles an hour is much to worry about."

"Maybe someday they'll get it to work better."

"I won't hold my breath. Anyway, who is going to invest in an unproven machine like that?"

Henrietta laughed. "OK, I'm Queen of the Sky."

"Much more than that, you saved Britain from the Armada and stopped the war by kidnapping the kaiser. Instead of wasting a fortune on war—a stupid war, I might add—and preventing the killing of who knows how many thousands, we have peace and prosperity."

"Others could have done all that maybe and—"

Connie grinned and said, "And then again, maybe not."

"I still don't think I made that much difference."

"Just your being you made a difference."

"I think you are looking at me the same way you look at the stars and see things that aren't there."

"First off, there are things out there even if you can't see them. And I see the same things in you that a lot of people see, even if you can't see them yourself."

"Like what?

"To begin with, you've changed the way people see others. Even my mother's friends are learning their servants' names. You've shamed people into being nicer to each other."

"You are just being silly."

"Past that, thanks to your example, women will have the vote after the next election."

"You're giving me too much credit."

"I am not. And then there is the most important thing."

"And just what is that?"

"Without you, who could I have found who would make me as happy as you do?"

"Oh, I don't know. Some of those girls your mother was pushing on you… they seemed nice."

"Now who is being silly?"

"I'll stop." Connie took his wife in his arms and said, "Just consider what my cold, lonely life would have been staring up at the stars without you." That got him a kiss.

"I suppose you are correct." She kissed him again.

There was a knock on the door. Henrietta pulled back. "Come."

It was her aide-de-camp, Flight Commander Pierce. He said, "Your Grace, I hate to interrupt, but there's a message. We have a mission." He held out a piece of paper.

Henrietta took the paper and read it. "Thank you, Mr. Pierce. Tell Captain Truscott to set course."

Connie looked at his wife. "What's going on? Where are we going?"

"Does it matter?"

Connie smiled. "No, my dear, it does not. Of all the places we could go, so long as we are together, it is exactly where I want to be. But I do think your next adventure with a Cimarron will have to wait until morning. I have other plans for you tonight. After all, this is our honeymoon trip."

The End

CPSIA information can be obtained
at www.ICGtesting.com
Printed in the USA
LVHW080504110319
610180LV00031B/767/P